10851982

UCT 16 2018

NOPL@CICERO
8686 KNOWLEDGE LANE
CICERO, NY 13039

A Calf Named
Brian Higgins

A Calf Named
Brian Higgins

AN ADVENTURE IN RURAL KENYA

KRISTEN BALL

ONE ELM
BOOKS

Egremont, Massachusetts

ONE ELM
BOOKS

One Elm Books is an imprint of Red Chair Press LLC
Red Chair Press LLC   PO Box 333   South Egremont, MA 01258-0333
www.redchairpress.com

Publisher's Cataloging-In-Publication Data
(Prepared by The Donohue Group, Inc.)

Names: Ball, Kristen. | Sachs, Jeffrey, writer of supplementary textual content.
Title: A calf named Brian Higgins : an adventure in rural Kenya / Kristen Ball ; foreword
by Jeffrey D. Sachs, Director, Millennium Villages Project.

Description: South Egremont, MA : One Elm Books, an imprint of Red Chair Press
LLC, [2018] | Interest age level: 008-013. | Includes resources for young people
to follow up and take action to help with sustainable development. | Includes
bibliographical references. | Summary: "Thirteen-year-old Hannah Higgins is
convinced her summer is ruined when she is forced to travel to Africa and work in
a remote village in Kenya with her mom and uncle ... Just when she thinks nothing
could make this trip any worse, she learns people there are dying of hunger and
preventable disease. Hannah becomes frustrated and wants to help ... "--Provided by
publisher.

Identifiers: LCCN 2017908297 | ISBN 978-1-947159-00-6 (library hardcover) |
ISBN 978-1-947159-01-3 (paperback) | ISBN 978-1-947159-02-0 (ebook)

Subjects: LCSH: Teenage girls--Travel--Kenya--Juvenile fiction. | Volunteers--Kenya-
-Juvenile fiction. | Hunger--Kenya--Juvenile fiction. | Kenya--Social conditions--
21st century--Juvenile fiction. | CYAC: Teenage girls--Travel--Kenya--Fiction. |
Volunteers--Kenya--Fiction. | Hunger--Kenya--Fiction. | Kenya--Social conditions-
-21st century--Fiction.

Classification: LCC PZ7.1.B355 Ca 2018 (print) | LCC PZ7.1.B355 (ebook) | DDC
[Fic]--dc23

This book is a work of fiction. Any references to historical events, real people or real
places are used fictitiously. Other names, characters, places, and events are products of
the author's imagination, and any resemblance to actual events, places, or persons, living
or dead is entirely coincidental.

Text copyright © 2019 by Kristen E. Ball

Jacket illustration © 2019 by Laura Jacobsen

All rights reserved, including the right of reproduction in whole or in part in any form.
For permissions, contact publisher at info@redchairpress.com.

For information about special discounts for bulk purchases, please contact
Lerner Special Sales at 1-800-328-4929.

Map illustrations: iStock

Photos credit: All photos by the author

Printed in Canada
0718 1P FRNF18

MIX
Paper from
responsible sources
FSC® C016245

For all our friends in Kenya.

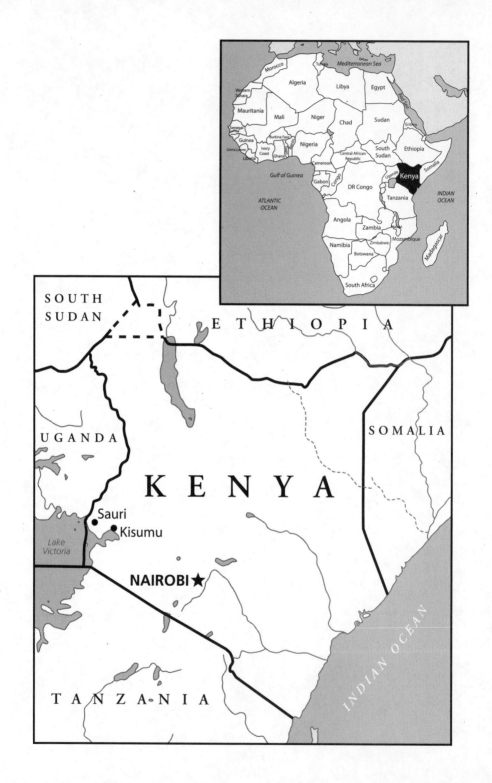

FOREWORD

*A*sante sana, Kristen Ball. Thank you so much. With *A Calf Named Brian Higgins,* you have made rural Africa come alive for young readers everywhere. And with heart, humor, and excitement, you've described how people can reach across the world to enrich the lives of others.

The book is captivating for young readers and their teachers and parents alike. If it all seems vivid and thrilling, it's because Kristen Ball has lived it. She knows of what she writes. With verve, smarts, and a huge heart, Kristen Ball herself worked in Sauri, Kenya, the first of the Millennium Villages, to bring computers and connectivity to the community. As a teacher in the US and a volunteer in Sauri, she has been one of the pioneers of using information technology to connect African and American children in the real key to globalization: direct and joyous contacts in an Internet-empowered global classroom!

Amazingly, Kristen Ball has done it all: weaving a captivating story, describing the trials and tribulations of extreme poverty, and most impressively, conveying the reality of progress now reaching across Africa. She tells the story of an impoverished village entering the information age, mobilizing medicines and bed nets to fight malaria, and reducing chronic hunger with improved agricultural practices. But she does not sugarcoat poverty. With sensitivity she conveys just how precarious life can be when water is unsafe, clinics are undersupplied, and transport, communications, and electricity are all unreliable. Yes, as she says, "everything is possible," yet real progress requires commitment and goodwill, the key lesson of this wonderful book.

Most importantly, Kristen Ball has crafted a true-to-life story about our common humanity, how goodwill transcends continents, languages, lifestyles, income levels, and life histories. In our globalized world, where connections are just the click of a button or an airplane trip right away, we have much to teach each other, and much to benefit from deepening our understanding and appreciation of the lives of others. This will be an unforgettable start to that process for countless young people who will treasure this wonderful story.

Jeffrey D. Sachs

Jeffrey D. Sachs is a world-renowned professor of economics, leader in sustainable development, senior UN advisor, and bestselling author. He is the director of the UN Sustainable Development Solutions Network for the Secretary General for the UN. Sachs is co-founder and Chief Strategist of Millennium Promise Alliance, and is director of the Millennium Villages Project.

He is the co-recipient of the 2015 Blue Planet Prize, the leading global prize for environmental leadership. He has twice been named among Time Magazine's 100 most influential world leaders. He was called by the New York Times, "probably the most important economist in the world," and by Time Magazine "the world's best known economist." A recent survey by The Economist Magazine ranked Professor Sachs as among the world's three most influential living economists of the past decade.

Landing in Nairobi

"Who comes all the way to Africa without a Plan B?" Hannah grunted and rolled her eyes at her mom. After fifteen hours of flying, she was exhausted. And her stomach still ached from the turbulence. *Maybe I should have listened to Dad and stayed home.* She wanted to cry. *My stomach is killing me. I need a ginger ale.*

Her Uncle Brian who lived and worked in Kenya was supposed to pick them up at the airport and was not there. "What are we going to do now?" Hannah asked. Her mom sighed. She took a step closer to Hannah and put her arm around her. With one swift roll of her shoulder, Hannah pushed her mom off. She tilted her head to the side and raised her eyebrows as far up her forehead as they would go. Through her flared nostrils she exhaled an exaggerated breath and started tapping her foot on the tile floor.

Scanning the room for her uncle, Hannah noticed she and her mom—the only white people in the Nairobi Jomo Kenyatta International Airport—stood out like two small children lost in Times Square in New York City. Her white skin made her feel more uncomfortable than afraid. People rushed by. She stopped tapping her foot and observed. Men were dressed in short sleeved button-down untucked shirts with loose-fitting lightweight pants and black rubber sandals. All the colors of their clothes were plain. There were very few women in the airport. Unlike the colors the men wore, the women wore vibrantly patterned dresses, mostly large floral prints, and black rubber sandals. Seeing her reflection in the glass divider at customs made Hannah gasp. She looked down at her clothes—a white short-sleeved t-shirt, a long navy skirt that reached the floor, and orange and blue Asics running sneakers—bothered by how much she stood out. She adjusted her tortoiseshell eyeglasses and tried to ignore her nervousness. Her mom, who seemed oblivious to everything, hustled her along to the desk to purchase visas.

Without expression, the male employee at the counter said, "US Passport and US fifty dollar." Her mom handed him Hannah's passport and $50. He looked Hannah up and down, reviewed her passport and handed it to her. Hannah smiled and thanked him. He nodded, put the money in a drawer and repeated, "US Passport and US fifty dollar." She watched her mom hand him her passport and another $50. He returned her passport and waved them forward. Her mom thanked him and walked ahead like a Pointer dog in search of the perfect spot to bury its bone. Hannah rolled her eyes and sighed, and followed her mom, who looked back every two seconds even though Hannah was right behind her.

There was still no sign of Uncle Brian. They looked through the windows to the outside. Unmarked black cars resembled gypsy cabs Hannah had seen in New York City. Her parents had warned her they were illegal and never to take them no matter how long the wait was for a yellow cab. Her mom tried to put her arm around Hannah and she pulled away again, but this time not too far. It was dark outside and Uncle Brian was still not answering his phone. Outside the airport there were even more strangers and probably fewer people who spoke English. For the first time since they had left home, Hannah nestled in close to her mom.

A man approached them holding a sign, HIGGINS. He had dark skin and his short hair was black with white flecks. In a soft, accented voice, he said, "Meredith Higgins."

She looked at Hannah. *What do you want me to do? I don't know who this guy is.* She felt her heart skip a beat and hoped her mom would handle it.

Shifting her gaze from Hannah to the stranger, her

mom answered. "Yes." Her voice trailed up as she spoke, like she was answering his question with a question. In that moment, the Pointer dog had become an innocent puppy.

The man handed her an envelope. She took Hannah by the upper arm, positioned her where she could see her and opened the envelope. Her face lost its color and her skin looked even paler next to the dark skin of the African man. She handed the stranger her duffel and grabbed Hannah's hand so hard that this time she could not pull it away. Truth be told, she did not want to.

Uncle Brian and the Zinc Lady

"What's the matter? Where's Uncle Brian?" Hannah sat close to her mom in the back of one of the same unmarked cars she had been taught to avoid at all costs. *See, Mom? She wanted to say. We're in what's probably the same exact thing as a gypsy cab and everyone is still alive.*

"He's stuck on the road somewhere. His bus broke down on its way here. This man is going to take us to a hotel for the night and we'll go to Kisumu tomorrow."

As they drove, it looked a lot like New York City— bright lights and tall buildings. Streets were crowded with people. "Oh," Hannah said. Feeling better with a plan, she reached into her backpack and got out a half-eaten bag of Sour Patch Kids. "Why didn't you just tell me that in the first place? What's the big deal?" She groaned. "You're so frantic." She ate some candy and glared at her mom but kept her thoughts to herself. *You always mess everything up. At least Dad's not here. Uncle Brian is going to show me around and take me to buy some cool Maasai bead jewelry.*

It was after midnight by the time they checked in to Room 312 of the Intercontinental Hotel. Hannah had no idea what time it would be at home and was too tired to do the simple math. She got out a brush and started combing through her knotted hair. It felt so good to get a brush through it. No more tangles. Just the softness she was used to. Pulling out her long brown strands of hair from the brush, she realized she had lost her hair elastic sometime during the last leg of her trip, but she had plenty more, a pack of assorted colors. She grabbed a green one and tied her hair back into a ponytail.

She stumbled into the tiny bathroom with her toiletry bag—light pink with white polka dots—and turned on the sink faucet. A thin stream of water flowed. She twisted the knob as far as it would go, but the pressure did not change. She could still feel the film from the soap on her face and hands when she climbed into bed.

As tired as she was, she could not sleep. Her parents' harsh words to each other from the night before she and her mom left for Kenya were still fresh in her mind. She heard her mom's voice, her emphasis centering on the pronouns like darts hitting a bulls-eye. *He's **your** brother, Dan. **You** should be going, not **me**. I take that back. **I** am* *happy to be taking **our** daughter to fulfill the promise **we** made to **your** brother.*

Just as sharp, her dad fired back. *The promise we made? We? I never promised to do anything.*

Of course you didn't. You never would. You're too selfish.

I'm selfish? You're the one dragging Hannah because you want to go. Brian thinks he can change the world, Meredith. *He can't. Poverty has been around forever and it always will be. It's bad enough right here in the US. In Africa, it's worse. No one person is going to change that, not anywhere.*

You're just too closed-minded to see that even if what Brian's doing helps save one life, he's making a difference.

Oh, stop. You sound like one of those syrupy clips on the news. And what do you know about it anyway? You've never been to one of those places. And how's this all going to work, Meredith? *Now you're going to save the world? Make a difference? You and Hannah?*

Yes, Dan. *We are.*

Hannah remembered sitting in her bedroom holding her Tibetan Terrier, Livvy, and listening intently. She wanted to rush to her mom and side with her. But part of her agreed with her dad. And throughout the years she had learned it was best to stay out of it anyway.

There was a knock at her bedroom door. She heard her dad's voice. "Hannah? Can I come in?" His gentle tone made her crazy. *He can be so fake. Does he really think I didn't just hear that whole conversation?*

7   CHAPTER 2

"Yes," she muttered.

"It's not too late to decide you don't want to go. You can stay here. It's your summer vacation from school, after all." *They always want me to choose between them. It's like he's saying, 'Pick me! Pick me!'* "Mom's been obsessed with this trip since Uncle Brian started working in Africa," he grumbled. "In her Peace Corps days after college, she never had the courage to travel so she stayed and worked in the home office. She feels like now is her chance. But you'll have other chances, if you decide you ever want to go." His voice was slick like when salespeople get too pushy trying to sell stuff.

Hannah hated when her parents made their problems into her problems. And she hated that she did not want to go and wanted to go at the same time. She felt like her mom in her "Peace Corps days."

"What about Uncle Brian? I already told him I was going." *He's the only reason I want to go.* "And weren't the plane tickets like a million dollars?"

"Uncle Brian will understand. And no, the ticket wasn't a million dollars." He chuckled. "It was a few thousand, but it's a refundable ticket, Hannah, so it's your choice. Think about it and we can talk more in the morning." He kissed her on the top of her head and walked out.

The pressure to choose whether or not to go—to choose between her parents—consumed her. She wished she could be half as relaxed as her dog, belly up and snoring on her bed beside her. Her dad was right. It was her summer vacation and she wanted to be with her friends. But she loved adventures and her uncle. She lay down next to Livvy and thought of the last time Uncle Brian had visited.

She had been sent to her room for lying to her parents about unfinished homework. Sitting on the top step of the staircase with her elbows resting on her knees and her chin propped up in her hands, she listened to them playing $25,000 Pyramid downstairs. Her mom gave clues. "Lace. Piping. Mexico. Canada. Fringe."

Unable to resist having the answer, Hannah called out, "Borders!"

She expected loud cheers. Instead, there was silence.

"Want to play?" Uncle Brian broke the tension. He got up off the couch, leaned his head up the staircase, winked at her and smiled. "You got it, so you're up!" They played for the rest of the afternoon and somehow she was no longer in trouble.

After dinner, her mom was making tea. Hannah excused herself from the table and said she still had one more test to study for.

"Want me to quiz you?" Uncle Brian asked.

"Sure," Hannah answered. "It's in science. Not my favorite subject and I don't really like the teacher."

"Why not?"

"Because she says things like, 'I zinc you know the answer!'"

Uncle Brian laughed. "That's hilarious. Come on, she sounds funny."

Hannah continued defending her case. "She has a poster on the wall that says, 'Think like a proton and stay positive.'"

Brian laughed harder. "Well," he admitted, "that one's a little more questionable."

"She puts scratch-n-sniff stickers on our homework, and…" She burst out laughing.

"What?" Brian asked.

Hannah could not control herself. Tears streamed down her face. "There was this one time…" She could barely get the words out. "She puts the stickers on our homework."

"You said that already," Uncle Brian said, laughing. "And I have no idea what's so funny."

Hannah took a deep breath and waved her hands in front of her to refocus. "One time, we had all made mistakes on our homework." She started laughing again. "And she thought it would be funny to use stinky scratch-n-sniffs. And she chose poop." Fully crying with laughter at this point, she said, "And she had to dismiss us early because the whole room smelled so bad!" She wiped the tears from her eyes and caught her breath. "You're right," she said. "She actually is pretty funny."

The following morning Uncle Brian asked Hannah, "On a scale of one to ten, how much would it humiliate you if not only I drop you off at school, but I also go in and see the legendary zinc and poop lady?"

Hannah laughed. "Ten is the most humiliating?"

"Yes," Uncle Brian confirmed.

"Eleven."

He gave her a joking jab in the arm. "Seriously, Hannah, now that I know you're learning about the periodic table of the elements, I'm wondering if she's going to be teaching about water." He paused. "And I wanted to ask her if I can come in and talk to your class about access to clean water in places like Sauri."

"You mean like the wells being built in Africa that you told me about?"

"Yes, but there are wells being built all over," he explained. "And it's awesome. Because, you know, people can die from bacteria in water."

"Can't they just take antibiotics or something?" she asked.

"This is why I need to talk to Zinc." He leaned into Hannah. "I zinc I really do need to talk to her."

Hannah laughed. "You can talk to her, but I zinc you'll zinc she's crazy!"

As Uncle Brian had hoped, Hannah's teacher invited him back later that week to talk with the class about his work in Kenya. He looked at Hannah. "Scale of one to ten?"

"Five hundred!" She laughed. She leaned into him and whispered, "Just don't embarrass me, okay?"

"I zinc I will try not to," he whispered back.

Two days later and after a brief introduction by Hannah's teacher, Uncle Brian showed a slide with a picture of a boy wearing a dirty white button down shirt, a blue sweater with holes in it, and ripped blue shorts. He was smiling and holding a cell phone carved out of wood. Uncle Brian said, "This is Kiano. And he carved this cell phone himself." He pointed to the phone on the screen. "Look at the buttons."

Hannah looked around at her impressed classmates. She could hear them whisper, "That's so cool."

"Kiano and his friends have phones like this and talk to each other on them." He put a pretend phone up to his ear. "Allo?"

He took a step to the side and used his other hand to hold up a different pretend phone. "Ah, allo!"

The kids laughed.

"The kids there use wooden cell phones because there aren't many cell phones there. Yet. This is in Sauri, Kenya, where I live. I work for an organization in New York City and my job is to find solutions to help end poverty so people will have enough medicine, food, and clean water. And having cell phones will help people communicate with each other and others outside their community. I wanted you to see Kiano because he knows about cell phones and his family will likely get a cell phone before they have a toilet."

The class giggled. *I should have warned Uncle Brian we still act like five-year-olds sometimes.*

"Really?" He laughed. "Because I said, 'toilet'?"

The kids laughed harder. *You said it again.*

He looked at Hannah and she smiled and threw her hands up in the air. He shook his head. The boy sitting next to Hannah leaned over to her and whispered, "One cell phone for the whole family?"

Hannah shrugged her shoulders. "I guess so."

Uncle Brian continued talking. "More people in the world have a cell phone than a toilet."

The kids stopped laughing. The novelty of "toilet" had worn off.

"2.4 billion people—1 in 3—lack access to a toilet. And 663 million people—1 in 10—lack access to safe water."

Uncle Brian called on a student who said, "That means 10% of people in the world don't have safe water." The child paused. "That's a lot of people."

Another student called out. "And a third of the people in the world don't have a toilet?"

Uncle Brian nodded. He went on to talk about how many kids in Sauri, including Kiano—but more often girls than boys—need to walk a long way to get water each day sometimes instead of going to school. The class asked lots of questions and Uncle Brian answered them, including what can be done to help like getting toilets and proper waste removal systems, and building wells in places that need them.

The bell rang and nobody moved. "Oh, sorry, I can talk about this stuff forever." Uncle Brian said. "I'm really impressed. You know, Hannah's the best niece a guy could ask for." Pausing a moment, he added, "She's my only niece." He winked at her and laughed. "But seriously, she's awesome, and between her and having you guys as her friends, I am really hopeful for our future, I really am."

Hannah looked around. Everyone was smiling, including her teacher, who thanked Uncle Brian and whispered to Hannah, "I zinc you have a really special uncle." Hannah laughed. She looked over at Brian, who was smiling so big she knew he must have heard.

As the kids walked out to their next period class, she hugged her uncle and said, "Thanks, Uncle Brian. I love you."

"I love you, too, Hannah."

They looked at each other and said at the same time, "I zinc I really do."

Cuddling with Livvy in her bedroom, Hannah had made a decision. Over her summer vacation and her friends, and especially over her impossible parents, she chose her Uncle Brian. She was going to Sauri.

When the alarm went off at 5:00 a.m., Hannah felt more tired. She dragged herself into the shower and yelled out to her mom. "The shampoo isn't coming out of my hair! There is hardly any water at all!"

"Stand on your tip-toes and get your scalp as close to the showerhead as you can. That's what I did."

Great advice.

"And hurry up, Hannah. We need to get downstairs."

As they rushed through the lobby, her mom mumbled. "He said someone would be in the lobby around 5:30 a.m."

"Calm down, Mom." Hannah moaned. "And who's 'he'? Who's 'someone'? What are you talking about?" Her judgy eyes narrowed and even she recognized how she had lost all patience for her parents, especially her mother since she was the one right there. Hannah touched her ponytail, a mixture of her straight, fine hair and dried-out shampoo. It felt like a horse's ungroomed tail.

A short black man wearing black pants, a maroon button-down shirt and a black blazer walked through the double glass doors into the lobby. His salt-and-pepper hair was cut very short and his soft brown eyes were friendly. He smiled. "Higgins?"

"Yes," her mom answered with more trust this time. He handed them two airline tickets, took the duffel from Hannah and led them outside to his car.

Meeting Sarah Oloo

Back in the same airport just over six hours after they had left, Hannah and her mom were disheveled. They hustled toward the East African Safari Air gate where they had learned they were scheduled to be on the hour-long 7:45 a.m. flight from Nairobi to Kisumu. Waiting in line at the security check, Hannah noticed how ancient the machinery appeared. It was so old and seemed to beep randomly. Studying the dozen people in front of her and the crowd of people forming a line behind her, she made it to the front of the line and hoisted the bags up to the belt.

"You must pay." The security employee looked at Hannah's mother. "600 Kenyan Shillings." Hannah and her mom looked at each other and then, at the same time, at the duffel. The security guard continued, "Weight limit

10 kilogram. Your bag weigh 20 kilogram." He handed them back their tickets and explained, "You need go." Without looking up at them, he waved his hand toward a set of counters off to the side. "Pay overage fee and come back at me for boarding pass." They did not have any local currency with them.

Hannah's mom grabbed the duffel and hurried in the direction the man had pointed. Hannah waited. She saw a baggage employee stop her panicked mother and direct her the opposite way. She shook her head and sighed. She felt kind of bad for her mom who looked over to her. Hannah waved to let her know she was okay. The woman standing behind Hannah said, "You use my weight."

She was an African businesswoman who spoke with a local accent, wore a fuchsia blouse and navy blue suit, and carried only a black leather briefcase. On her way to Kisumu for a day of meetings, she explained, she had nothing but her briefcase.

Hannah called out to her mom explaining what the businesswoman had just told her. The security agent was quick to tell them that this was not allowed. As her mom raced back to the counter, the woman pleaded with the employee to "be kind." In response to her firm tone, the man obliged and handed them their boarding passes.

There was only one gate area with a few small tables and chairs, and a refreshment stand with fruit, bottled water, bread and hot tea. Hannah's mom looked at her new friend and said, "Thank you. May I get something for you for being so kind to us?"

"Hot tea would be wonderful," the woman replied.

Hannah followed her mom and asked, "What about me? Do I get anything?" She felt like a brat needing her mom's full attention. But she did.

"Of course," her mom insisted. She pointed to a sign behind the counter that US currency was accepted and smiled. "But I don't think we should have the fruit here." She leaned into Hannah and whispered, "It might not be fresh." Hannah rolled her eyes and asked for bread and water. *This is what they serve in jail.* They purchased their food and walked back to the table to join Sarah Oloo. Hannah took a bite of bread and zoned out.

"Hannah?" Her mom's voice startled her. "Did you hear? Sarah Oloo is the Chief Architect of the Ministry of Roads and Public Works for all of Kenya."

Hannah wondered if she was supposed to be impressed.

"She's going to look up Sauri as soon as she gets back to her office tomorrow."

"Cool," Hannah said, uninterested. She ate the last piece of her bread.

Hannah felt herself becoming irritated by the way Sarah Oloo treated Hannah's mom like a red carpet movie star. Sarah batted her eyes and grinned so hugely that Hannah wondered how her jaw did not hurt. She asked questions about New York and used "New York" and "America" interchangeably, making Hannah question whether the woman knew the difference or was just too starry-eyed to pay attention to details.

Hannah got out her bag of Sour Patch Kids and popped a few in her mouth. Sarah Oloo's eyes grew three sizes like the Grinch's heart at Christmas. She stared at the package of candy. Hannah scrunched her nose and asked, "You want one?"

She giggled like a little girl. Hannah handed her the pack. *There are only three left. Go for it.*

"Asante, asante!"

Hannah forced a grin. *I have no idea what you're saying.*

An African man walked to each of the tables telling people that it was time to board the plane to Kisumu. Hannah looked out the window and saw the small plane.

Wait a minute. Her stomach turned. *She's the person in charge of roads in Kenya and she's never even heard of Sauri?*

East African Safari Air

Hannah sat on the aisle. A piece of thick silver duct tape held up the tray table of the seat in front of her. She looked around. *Is this plane even safe?* Sarah Oloo walked by them and took her seat a few rows back.

What could possibly be the reason for her not knowing Sauri? She thought back to the previous night when they had paid $50 cash each for a visa. *Where does that money go? We didn't even get a visa. What is a visa?* She was so drained, it seemed as though that was weeks ago.

They were buckled in and ready for departure. *At least the seatbelts are secure. And duct tape is pretty strong stuff.* Hannah leaned over and asked her mom, "Where do you think the $50 goes?"

"What $50?"

"The $50 they charged us for our visas." Hannah made air quotes with her fingers as she said the word, "visa."

"I'm not sure. Why?"

"Because your new best friend over there works for the Kenyan government and hasn't even heard of Sauri. Doesn't that seem strange to you? Think about it."

"Hannah." Her mom sounded exasperated. "Stop being so rude. You've been terrible to me since we got here." She looked over her shoulder to where Sarah Oloo was seated and looked back at Hannah. "But you do have a point."

Hannah and her mom exited the plane in Kisumu and followed the line of passengers out onto the runway where they waited for their bags. The single runway was next to a small, enclosed room that was the Kisumu Airport. Sarah Oloo did not have a bag to retrieve, but walked up to Hannah and her mom, wished them a good trip to Sauri, and left.

"See!" her mom said, putting her hands on her hips. "She said, 'Sauri.'"

"So what?" Hannah asked.

"So now she knows about it."

Hannah shook her head. "Big deal," she said under her breath.

A young African man with a huge smile wearing a baseball cap, Levi's jeans and a navy blue t-shirt stood behind a chicken wire fence between the runway and the airport. He held a sign, HIGGINS.

CHAPTER 4

"Jambo!" he exclaimed. He walked toward them and shook their hands. The only white people on the flight, Hannah groaned when everyone immediately knew who they were. She wanted to fit in.

The three of them walked just a few yards and reached a yellow Toyota pickup truck. The man put the duffel and their backpacks in the back. He opened the passenger side door and introduced himself. "I am Jones."

Hannah gasped. "You're Jones? Uncle Brian talks about you all the time!"

"Hannah, I know many stories to you, too." She smiled. "And I take you first to Classic Guest House where you stay in Kisumu. Patrick meet us there."

Patrick, a middle-aged Kenyan, worked at the World Agroforestry Center in Kisumu, which they referred to as ICRAF, to help build agricultural and sustainability programs in developing nations. Uncle Brian worked closely with him.

"Is Uncle Brian meeting us, too?" Hannah asked, distracted by all of the passengers waiting for their bags. Her mind trailed off. She wondered if the Maasai people in Kenya made beaded belts. She knew she wanted at least one for herself and thought they would make cool gifts to take to her friends back home. She thought about how much they might cost and how many would fit in her bag, which she had purposely under-packed to leave room for stuff to buy there and take home.

Jones looked at them. "Yes, yes. I sorry I not tell you before. Brian, he is fine. He get stuck on bus to Nairobi. It break down and he have no cell phone battery. But he call Patrick and Patrick get you here to Kisumu and to ICRAF."

Hannah's mom let out a long sigh. "That's what the note said but I wasn't sure what was going on. Why didn't he just call me?" She looked at Hannah. "Or you?"

"Uh, because you kept my cell phone for some reason." *Because you're a hoarder and don't want me to use up data. And you don't understand that texting my friends uses no data anyway.* "And he probably doesn't know our numbers."

"How can he not know our numbers? They're in his cell phone."

Hannah shrugged, exasperated by her mom's lack of tech savvy. "But he can't look them up if he has no battery. Ugh."

"Oh, right," her mom realized.

Jones explained. "Brian call Patrick because he know number to ICRAF center. He maybe be back at Classic when we get there." *He understood way more of our conversation than I thought he would.* Her cheeks blushed.

As they climbed into the truck, the intensity of the sun and the thickness of the red clay dust that smelled like manure and burning plastic permeated the air and made Hannah feel nauseated. She caught a glimpse of her eyes in the massive rearview mirror and was startled by their appearance, a blend of hazel green and scarlet red. She blinked hard to focus her vision and tears formed. Providing moisture and relief to the stinging, they looked like little rivers flowing down along the thick dust on her face. She took off her glasses momentarily and used the back of her hand to wipe the tears from her cheeks and the inside of her t-shirt to remove the smudgy dirt from her lenses.

She put her glasses back on and searched the front seat of the truck for seatbelts but did not find any. The three of them were to sit across the front seat of the car—without seatbelts—driving on unpaved roads. *This is worse than duct tape holding together seats on a plane.* Hannah looked up at Jones. "There aren't seatbelts?"

His big brown eyes were gentle. "Do not worry, Hannah. I am careful driver," he assured her and turned the key in the ignition.

Classic Guest House

A short, pudgy African woman dashed toward them, her arms wide open and ready for a hug, with a smile that matched Jones's in its enormity. *How is everyone here so happy all the time? It's so dirty. There are no seatbelts. Uncle Brian is stranded on some broken-down bus somewhere.*

"Hannah!" she hugged her. "I am Grace!" Hannah's glasses shifted and she bumped her nose as her face pressed against the woman's cheek and she was enveloped by her girth. The woman took a step back, held Hannah by the shoulders and looked at her. "You exactly like Brian say. Only so taller. Taller than me!" She laughed.

Before Hannah could speak, she heard a dog barking. "That is Ash," Grace said. Hannah looked down and saw a wiry haired Dachshund mutt running toward her. She squatted and he jumped into her lap, wagging his tail and licking her cheeks. She smiled and scratched his ears. *Even the dogs here are happy.* It seemed contagious.

Grace Mutuo, manager of the Classic Guest House in Kisumu, had known Uncle Brian for years, first as a patron and then as a close friend. Hannah had heard from her uncle about his long conversations with Grace, how he loved her like a big sister, a faraway friend he considered family.

Grace led Hannah and her mom to the office of the Classic Guest House while Jones waited. The dog trotted happily alongside them. Hannah thought of her dog, Livvy, at home and probably feasting on a bone, begging for cheese at the refrigerator, or "helping" her dad prepare a meal in the kitchen. She missed them. And in a place near where there was no electricity or running water, where people were dying of hunger and disease, she had been worried that animals may be suffering as well, but not Ash. Well-fed and spoiled with affection, Ash went everywhere with Grace.

All of the rooms at the Classic Guest House had an outside entrance. Grace escorted them from the office up a set of chipped white painted stairs. "This Brian's room." She walked a few steps forward and opened the next door. "And this your room. I hope is okay."

The room was painted white and had a wooden chair in the far left corner. Next to it a full-size bed under a large white net cascaded down in a cone shape from a circular fixture attached to the ceiling. There was a plain wooden bureau with three drawers to the right of the bed and a bathroom off to the side.

"Yes, Grace, this is perfect. Thank you. We'll just take a few minutes up here to get settled and we'll be down soon."

"Is okay, yes. Is good." She touched Meredith's arm and walked back downstairs, Ash beside her.

Hannah walked into the bathroom. She turned the faucet knob. Dribbles spat into the sink. She waited for the water pressure to flow. The dribbles stopped. She turned the knob off. Then back on. Nothing.

"Can I use the toilet if there's no water?" She asked her mom.

"It won't flush," her mom warned. *Gross*. She thought back to Uncle Brian's visit to her science class. *He talked about more people having cell phones than toilets. He never said anything about the people with toilets that don't work. That's a whole new category.*

She dragged the massive duffel toward the bed and unzipped it. "Now that we're here, I feel much better. All I want is to splash cold water on my face—I guess I'll do that later—and go for a quick run." She searched for her running gear and pulled out leggings, a sports bra, and a t-shirt. "I still can't believe I have to cover my shoulders and legs here just because I'm a female. We're not living in the Middle Ages. And we still stick out like a sore thumb anyway."

"Hannah, you can't go for a run," her mom declared.

"I need to get out of here," she pleaded. "At least for a minute. I want to get a big bottle of water and see if I can find some more Sour Patch Kids or something. Can I have some money?" She thought about which direction to go and realized she had not seen any stores.

"Hannah, you can't just go out by yourself here," her mom reiterated. "And remember we brought peanut butter crackers and protein bars. They're in my backpack if you want them." She started unpacking her things. "Just wait until Uncle Brian gets here, okay?"

"Did I hear someone call my name?" Uncle Brian opened the door.

"Uncle Brian!" Hannah exclaimed. She ran into his arms and hugged him.

"I'm so sorry about last night," he said. "That was crazy. The bus broke down. We were stranded. ICRAF had lost power before I left, so my cell phone wasn't charged. What a mess."

Hannah's mom greeted him with a hug. "Don't worry. We were fine."

Not wanting her uncle to feel bad about not being there, Hannah added, "Someone was there to pick us up at the airport last night and from the hotel this morning. And we even met someone while waiting for the flight here." She looked at her mom. "Remember the lady who ate all my Sour Patch Kids? Sarah Oloo?"

Uncle Brian interrupted. "You met Sarah Oloo? You're kidding me."

"You know her?" Meredith asked.

"Yes, of course. We've met a bunch of times. She's the Chief Architect of the Ministry of Roads and Public Works for all of Kenya."

"She didn't even know Sauri." Hannah grunted. Noticing her uncle's deflated expression, she backpedaled. "I mean, she did know Sauri in the end, right, Mom?" Her mom nodded. "She said to enjoy our time in Sauri, didn't she, Mom?"

"Yes, Hannah, that's right." She looked at Uncle Brian. "She did say that, Brian."

He attempted a smile. "I don't care if she knows me or not. I just want her to remember our meetings about improving roads around here and starting to build them out toward Sauri." He jokingly nudged Hannah. "Maybe I should bring Sour Patch Kids to my next meeting with her, huh?"

"Yeah, she really liked them!" Hannah said and then changed the subject. "Uncle Brian, will you go for a run with me? And I want to get some more candy or something. And a water."

"Sure, let's go. But we won't run. We'll take a boda-boda."

"We'll take a what?" She giggled.

Boda-Bodas

Grace offered hot tea to Meredith who was still looking pale and had decided to stay back with Grace and rest while Hannah and Uncle Brian went off to explore Kisumu. Hannah was thrilled to get a break from her mom. For the first time since she left her home, she felt free.

"So what are boda-bodas?"

Uncle Brian looked at Hannah and explained. "So you're supposed to hop on the back of these old, rusty bikes and let a young Kenyan pedal you around. There's a little, and I mean *little*, cushion on the back, and you're literally supposed to hop right on in one smooth motion so the bike doesn't tip and the poor guy riding the bike doesn't pull a muscle. You'll see in a minute.

"Zaidi ya hapa tafadhali!" he called out and continued

talking to Hannah who took a deep breath and smiled with her mouth wide open, taking in her new surroundings and savoring every moment. "The first time I rode on one, I hopped on the bike smoothly—or what I thought was smoothly—trying to fit in but really just making more of a spectacle of myself, and we almost crashed into a cart of oranges! The guy tried to steady the bike and then I shifted my weight to help and we almost fell over again! He stopped and I apologized. He kept saying, 'Is okay,' and motioned for me to get off. He stood the bike stationary and motioned for me to get back on. I had to get on first! I felt like I was riding a bike without training wheels for the first time. It was humiliating," he said, laughing. "You have to picture that everyone hops on and off these things all the time, for short rides, longer rides, and for me, he had to stop the bike and have me get on first. Then, as he was pedaling, he was heaving. He didn't mean to, I don't think, but the bike was creaking and the poor guy was heaving. I thought, 'Did I eat too much nyoyo last night?'" He patted his stomach.

Hannah laughed out loud. "Wait, is that going to happen to me? What's nyoyo?"

A thin African man, probably in his late teens, rode up to them on his bike. "Boda-boda?" he asked. Hannah was thrilled. Brian used his index and middle finger to indicate they would like two. The man called out something in words Hannah did not understand and within moments one of his buddies showed up on his bike.

Chapter 6

Hannah climbed on the back of the first bike. She said, "Jambo!" to the guy riding. Uncle Brian had taught her that Swahili word when she was little so she knew it meant, "Hello!"

He smiled and said, "Jambo," back to her. Uncle Brian told the young men where they were going, and off they went, riding to the side of the dirt path in case of passing traffic of which there was none. Hannah wobbled a bit on the back, but held her abs tight, her body upright, and—for a moment—held her breath, and once they were steadied, she relaxed. As the guy pedaled, she heard him breathing heavily as the old bike squeaked along. She thought of Uncle Brian having eaten too much nyoyo and giggled. She still did not even know what nyoyo was.

The sudden stench of body odor made her gag. As the man pedaled faster, the movement in the still air created ripples in his shirt and the scent became stronger. She looked down at her shirt. It was just as dirty as his. And she had not had a good shower since she left the United States. *The smell could definitely be me.* They had only pedaled a short while and yet it seemed they were in a completely different place. Although it was still Kisumu, there were more cars and there were also dozens of matatus—psychedelic colored hippie buses carrying loads of people and honking their horns. Vendors with old, antique-looking wooden carts sold bananas, oranges, and bags of flour. There were some with loaves of bread. Nearby, large sticks fashioned into posts were lined up in rows with a large, colorful fabric overhang. Underneath were cotton sheets spread across the dirt, displaying masses of wooden crafts and toys.

They got off the bikes and Uncle Brian paid the riders.

Uncle Brian bought some fruit and bread to take back to the Classic while Hannah waited to peruse the goods under the tent. She looked around. They were the only white people in the market. She had never paid much attention to her skin color, and this was the third time in two days she had noticed it. She moved closer to her uncle. "Can you stay with me, Uncle Brian?" she asked, looking around.

"Of course." He paused, confused by her request. "What do you mean?" He stopped, observed her overwhelmed expression, and understood. He put his arm around her. "We're sticking together forever, Hannah. Don't worry." She smiled. "See those baskets over there?" He pointed to a woven basket with bright pink, purple, and green trim. "My friends here gave one just like that to me so I can carry fruit at home. Can you imagine me walking around the streets of New York City with a basket of fruit on my head?" Hannah giggled.

"You never told me what nyoyo is."

"Oh, yeah. It's corn and beans."

Hannah made a face. "Yuck."

"No, no, it's so good! The kernels of maize are so big and the beans are delicious. You'll love it!" He licked his lips and paused. "Except this one time..." He had a twinkle in his eye. "I bit into a worm in the nyoyo that was juicy, too."

"Gross!"

"Boil it, peel it, or leave it! And—as they say—as long as it's cooked, it counts as protein!"

Hannah laughed. "Boil it, peel it, or leave it makes sense because of the bacteria in the water, but who would ever say about a worm that as long as it's cooked it counts as protein? Who says that?" She laughed harder. Nudging her in the arm, he laughed too.

They walked further into the market. "I think my mom isn't tired," she blurted out. "I think she's on stress and anxiety overload. Kind of the way I get with exams but worse. She was really nervous about coming here. And I don't want you to feel bad, but she really was upset last night at the airport when you weren't there." She hesitated and looked at the red dirt ground. "So was I." She caught herself and looked up at him to explain. "Not mad. Not mad at all, just worried. I mean, we know why you weren't there and it wasn't your fault."

He carried the fruit and bread in one arm and put his other around her as they walked. "Yeah," he agreed. "But she'll get used to it and so will you, I promise. And I know it is really important to her to be here. And to bring you."

Hannah nodded.

"How's your dad?"

"He's okay." Again, she recalled her parents' fight. She did not mention to Uncle Brian that her dad had said her mom only wanted to go in order to redeem herself and that poverty would never end. And she definitely did not want to admit that to him that she had her own doubts. "For brothers, you two sure are different."

Uncle Brian laughed. "We're more alike than you think." As Hannah raised an eyebrow and questioned his statement, she heard a catchy song in the distance. A group of local teenagers—one with a boom box—were nearby.

Hannah loved to dance. Her shoulders seemed to start moving on their own. "What's that song?"

Instead of answering, Uncle Brian leaned into Hannah and started singing mumbled words perfectly in tune. She laughed out loud. "You never know the words to songs!"

He laughed, too. "I know, but at least this one is mostly in Swahili, so it's not as obvious."

"But you still don't know the words."

"Not at all," he admitted. "But I do know it's called Swing Swing and all the kids here love it. So do I."

"So do I! I'll download it to my phone when I get it back from my mom." As she walked through the market with a spring in her step, Hannah asked, "Can we get some Maasai bead jewelry?"

"Sure! But hang on," he said. "There's a girl in Sauri I want you to meet. She's just about your age and makes really cool beaded bracelets. Her name is Wilkister and she's so funny and smart—just like you. Her grandmother does a lot of work with our community food program and takes care of her, her two brothers, and her little sister. Her parents both died. I never knew her mom but I knew her dad. They're such a good family."

"How did her parents die? That's so sad."

"Her mom died when she was giving birth to Wilkister's little sister. And her dad had typhoid. He died just last year."

Hannah looked down at the dirt ground. Uncle Brian continued talking. "But she is awesome and so are you! I told her all about you."

"You did?"

"Indeed I did! And she wants to teach you how to make the bracelets. What do you think?"

Hannah's eyes sparkled. "Yes!" she said. "I'd love that!"

"Cool," Uncle Brian said. "So let's wait on getting jewelry here. We can always come back."

Waiting with Great Expectations

Hannah and Uncle Brian took boda-bodas back to the ICRAF Center where they met up with Meredith, Jones, and Patrick. The ICRAF office—small and antiquated—had dusty chairs with ripped vinyl and padding showing through, a large wooden table, and several clunky, unreliable-looking desktop computers.

Patrick Oriwo managed the office and, like so many others Hannah and her mom had encountered in Kisumu, had a constant, genuine smile on his face. Hannah's theory that Kenyans are all happy people seemed a sweeping generalization at first but was quickly proving to be true. "Hannah!" he said as she and Uncle Brian walked in. "Welcome to Kenya!"

"Jambo, Patrick!" Having noticed people there shake hands every time they see each other, Hannah extended her right hand.

"We are so pleased you are here at Kisumu." He shook her hand and then Uncle Brian's, and then pointed his index finger over his lips to quiet everyone and motioned to Hannah to walk with him. Smiling and tiptoeing behind him, she looked to an adjacent room. Among cords and mismatched pieces of old technological equipment was Hector Sanchez who also worked with Uncle Brian and specialized in agricultural development. Hannah had met Hector before when he and Uncle Brian were at a meeting at the United Nations in New York City, not far from where she lived at home.

"Hannah!" Hector exclaimed when he spotted her. He picked her up and swung her around. As he put her down, he put his hands on her shoulders, looked deep into her eyes and enunciated in his thick Cuban accent, "The people of Sauri are waiting for you with great expectations."

Hannah smiled on the outside, but inside felt a pang in her stomach. *What expectations?* She looked up at Uncle Brian with raised eyebrows and wide eyes, and nestled into him. He put his arms around her.

Hannah's mom eyed the boxy desktop computers. "Do we have time to send a couple of quick e-mails? Our phones don't seem to be working." She looked over to Hannah. "And we need to call Dad." *That's code for "you need to call*

Dad."

Patrick looked at Hannah's mom. "We have electricity at the Center today," he pointed out and then gazed down at the floor. "But we do not have Internet today." His voice quieted, "Maybe tomorrow?" He did not seem sure.

"And I can help with your cell phones." Uncle Brian added. "Meredith, you're not going to be able to send emails or texts from here today—and definitely not out in Sauri—but we should be able to call Dan. If not with your phone, we can with mine."

Jones dropped Brian, Meredith, and Hannah back at the Classic and promised to be back in the morning to take them out to Sauri. Hannah looked to her left and right, leaned into Uncle Brian and whispered, "I smell really bad."

He sniffed. "You sure do!"

Hannah laughed. "No, really, I don't want Grace to hear me, but there was hardly any water at the hotel last night and there doesn't seem to be any at all here. Is there another place I can go to take a shower?"

"Sorry, Hannah. There really isn't. Sometimes there just isn't water." He called out to Grace. "Grace? Is there water today?"

She called back. "Water come tomorrow?" Hannah could not tell if that was a question or a statement. She was not sure if Grace knew either. And the promise of tomorrow loomed.

The mosquitoes hovered and seemed especially interested in the chicken and kale Grace prepared for dinner. The other guests—two college buddies who were backpacking through parts of East Africa during their summer vacation, a honeymooning couple on their way to safari at Maasai Mara, and a Japanese environmentalist exploring the nearby Kakamega Rainforest—were out on short trips and would not be back that evening, so it would be just the four of them. And Ash. And a thousand mosquitoes. Hannah ate her meal and drank bottled water that had become hot during the day. It was still hot at night.

Uncle Brian could not get their phones to work, so they used his—a sleek electric blue Motorola C116 with a SIM card that fit into the palm of Hannah's hand. It was new and shiny, unlike anything she had seen since she arrived in Kenya. She wondered how often her uncle was able to charge it. She would give him the portable chargers she and her mom brought so that his experience on the bus to Nairobi would not happen again. She hoped they would be compatible with his phone. She hoped they could get their phones to work at all.

Pressing the mini silver numbers on the keypad, she dialed home. When she placed it to her ear, the phone mouthpiece was only at the tip of her cheek. She felt like Inspector Gadget as she listened to the ringing and waited for her dad to pick up.

It was 7:00 p.m. local time, about noon back at home.

"Hello?"

"Hi, Dad!"

"Hi, Hannah!"

"How's Livvy?"

"She's right here beside me. It's almost lunchtime, after all." They both laughed.

There was a long pause. "Um, so we made it."

"Yes, that's great! How was the flight?"

"Good."

He broke the silence. "How's the weather?"

Of all the things to talk about, he asked about the weather. She could not stand it. "It's snowing," she said, rolled her eyes and handed the phone to her mother.

She went upstairs, reached for her backpack and unzipped it. She knew she was way too old to have brought a stuffed animal with her. She had been told in Sauri there would be no disease and hunger; no electricity, no running water, no medical supplies or clean water. And she had brought her stuffed bear she had named Beary. It was ridiculous, she knew. But in the end, she had brought him anyway. She got him out and curled up on the bed under the canopied net hugging him.

Her mom crawled in beside her. Hannah shifted her body away and fell asleep.

Land of No Return

Jones sat in the driver's seat while Hannah, Meredith, Brian, and Hector piled in next to him for the 45-minute drive to Sauri the following morning. With five people sandwiched across the front seat, Hannah felt more secure. They were squeezed so tightly that it almost did not matter that there were no seatbelts. Almost.

The dirt road became less and less uniform the further away they drove from Kisumu. The smell of farm animals and dust made her nostrils flare like those of the few cows they passed. Her filthy exterior resembled theirs. And she could see their ribs.

Hannah clutched the front seat. She did not like turbulence on planes or in cars. It did not help that vehicles in Kenya had the steering wheel on the right side and that they drove on the left side of the road. She closed her eyes to stop the motion, but her strategy did not work. She opened her eyes. The dashboard jostled. She looked straight through the dusty windshield. All the moving brown landscape made her nauseated. She looked down at her lap, her long navy skirt swaying back and forth; up and down. She closed her eyes again.

"Jones?" her voice boomed like Tarzan beating his chest with his hands. "Can we go a little faster? It might be less bumpy if we go faster."

"Oh, I sorry, Hannah," he said. "I cannot go faster. You soon see."

The roads worsened and Hannah clutched the seat again.

"We will pass equator," Jones announced.

Hannah opened one eye.

"Look out window at the right. You see a statue."

Though small, it appeared celestial, with four cement prongs holding up what looked like a circular mustard color planet with a red ring around it that read EQUATOR in white lettering. As they passed it, Hannah felt like she was crossing over into the land of no return.

She heard a beep, looked up at the windshield and saw a truck approaching them head-on. Sitting in between her mom and Uncle Brian, she grabbed their arms. Jones continued driving straight ahead and the approaching truck did the same. Hannah's sore eyes widened and she held her breath. They got closer. Her mom grabbed Hannah's hand and Uncle Brian put his arm across her body like a gate of protection. She screamed as Jones drove to the left, half off the road and half on, shifting the truck to a 45-degree angle to the ground. Just as quickly, he righted it. Gripping the arms of her mom and Uncle Brian, Hannah gasped and looked from person to person so quickly, she felt as though her head would spin right off her neck. "That was scary!" she yelled. Her mom shifted her body toward Hannah and hugged her. Hannah let out a breath, straightened her glasses, and got up on her knees to look behind her. The other truck was back up on the road driving along as if nothing had just happened. She sat back down and looked up at Jones. "Was that normal?" He nodded and out of the corner of her eye, Hannah noticed Uncle Brian give her mom a concerned look. *Is he worried about me? And where is this place?*

Uncle Brian informed them that they were just over halfway there, but still had about twenty minutes to drive on even rougher terrain to Sauri. Jones drove cautiously, weaving through the bumps, the truck up on its side, moving downward and upward like they were in a monster truck rally. Hannah held her breath hoping they would not get stuck, but as she became more and more carsick, she hoped maybe they would. They parked on dirt in front of an abandoned flour mill, the central meeting place in Sauri. It was 11:45 a.m. No one was there.

The stench of the air made Hannah unable to inhale fully. Her instinct was only to exhale. She looked around. A goat passed by. Two thin, mangy dogs trotted along. She thought of Livvy. A small pile of trash burned in the distance and smoke hung over it in the motionless air. The breaths Hannah took in were half the length of the breaths she was letting out. She began to feel lightheaded and walked into the flour mill to escape the outside reek, but it was worse inside.

There were two splintery plywood benches in a room with chipped walls and a tin slat roof, which exuded heat and let the sun beat inside through its unevenness. Hannah looked up and squinted her stinging eyes against the intensity of the white-hot sun. Dried beans and stalks of corn were piled in one corner. She looked through the back entrance, a tall rectangular hole in the wall. There were wilted corn stalks. A goat walked in the doorway and startled her. It was filthy. Hannah wanted to run to it and hug it around its neck, but she remained still. The goat stared at her, looked around the room and walked back out. Stifled by the smell, trying to escape the heaviness of the stink, she walked outside for relief and found the same uneasy air she had left moments earlier.

"People will arrive soon," Hector announced. *Does everyone else smell what I smell? Is anyone else having trouble breathing?* She looked over to her mom who looked just as uneasy as Hannah. The four of them sat on wooden chairs on the porch, under the overhang of tin slats that extended beyond the one room flour mill. They waited.

Hannah looked at her watch. It was 1:15 p.m.—an hour and a half after their arrival. Hannah looked in every direction into the nothingness of her surroundings.

"Um, Hector?" she probed.

"They will be here," he responded. Gazing out into the distance, he held his head high and proud. She wondered about the people who were waiting with great expectations and what those great expectations were, but did not say a word. She drank from her bottled water for relief from the heat, but it was hot, and in each mouthful of water she could taste the manure in the air. She studied the four bathroom stalls several yards from where they sat. The white paint with peacock-blue trim was chipped and dirty. She got up from her porch chair and walked toward them. Four painted doors side by side. She opened one and a mass of mosquitoes buzzed into her face. They stank of poop. She gasped and shrieked, and in one swift motion closed the door, turned her head and shielded her face in the crook of her elbow. Uncle Brian raced to her. "Are you okay?"

Her cheeks burned. "Yes," she said. "I'm sorry."

"Nothing to be sorry about," he responded. They walked to the back of the flour mill among the withered stalks and wandering goats. "There sure is a lot of poop around here, huh?"

She giggled. "There's poop all over the place! And

can't people aim into those holes a little better?" They both laughed.

"Just go in the stalks, Hannah." He waved his hand nonchalantly in the air and assured her. "You're good."

Sauri Clinic

"**L**et's walk to the clinic," Uncle Brian suggested. He looked over to Hector and Jones. "When the people arrive, please tell them we'll be back soon, okay?" The two men nodded and sat back down.

"I think I'll just rest here, too," Meredith said. "I'm tired." Hannah looked at her uncle. *See? She's not tired.* "Hannah, would you please take the bag of medicine?" She handed her the small duffel.

"Can't you just come with us?" Hannah tried to insist. Her mom shook her head.

Uncle Brian took the bag from Hannah and put his other arm around her. Kicking up dust as they walked, they headed along the dry earth toward the clinic. They passed two men and a woman heading toward the flour mill. The people were dirty, and their hands were dry and weathered, just like the skin on their faces. "Jambo," one of the men said. They all shook hands. Hannah caught herself starting to wipe her hand on her skirt and, in a swift motion, put it out to the side, as if to prove to everyone— including herself—she was unbothered by adding another layer of grime.

"You are headed to town?" Uncle Brian asked.

Town, Hannah thought. *An old flour mill and four adjoined bug- and poop-infested holes in the ground was their town.*

"Yes," they responded in soft voices. "We not see you there?"

"You will see us there in just a few minutes. We are going to the clinic and will be back."

"Ah, nzuri." The woman nodded and smiled. Her teeth were a yellowish brown color all along her gums. A few teeth had brown spots in the middle and along the bottom edge. They were rotting. "Asante sana." She waved as they continued walking.

"Karibu sana," Uncle Brian answered. He leaned into Hannah. "Africa time. You'll get used to it," he said, and winked. Hannah smiled. Despite the vastness of the land and the wide-open space, she stayed right beside her uncle.

As they continued along, Hannah noticed all that was missing. There were no street signs, no landmarks. There was nothing there. Absolutely nothing. She knew there would be no clothing or candy stores. She knew there would be no Starbucks, no shopping mall. But the desperate feeling of nothing to do overwhelmed her. There was nowhere to meet friends for an ice cream. No movie theater or library. No grocery store or bank.

And now this concept of Africa time was beginning to make sense. There was no rush because no one needed to get anywhere. No one needed to get anywhere because there was nowhere to go. Back home, Hannah would have given anything for free time. Free time from school, homework, cross-country practice, flute lessons. Sometimes she even wanted free time away from her friends. But with nothing to do and nowhere to go, her chest felt like she was trapped under a heavy piece of furniture. The thought of living this way day after day shocked her. She had trouble breathing again. And this time it was not all because of the stink in the air.

They approached a cement block room that was painted white and blue, the same colors of the bathroom stalls. The paint was chipped and dirty on this one-room building just as it had been on the bathrooms. "Sauri Clinic" was painted in black lettering above the front doorway—which had no door—so they walked in without knocking.

"Jambo, Dr. Omundo!" Uncle Brian exclaimed not seeming to notice the crowd of sickly people gathered around. Glassy eyes, yellow where they should be white. Skin with open wounds, rashes and sores. Mothers carrying crying babies on their backs in large colorful fabric wraps, weak people—young and old—holding each other up against the wall. A mixture of urine, dust and antiseptic filled the air. "This is my niece, Hannah Higgins." He sounded proud, which made Hannah happy.

Dr. Paul Omundo, a tall, handsome African man looking dignified in glasses and a white lab coat, stopped his treatment of a patient and looked up to greet them. "Jambo," he said and shook their hands. He was not wearing latex gloves.

Hannah reached into her mom's duffel and pulled out several large plastic bags filled with medicine and supplies. She handed them to the doctor. "These are from my mom," she said. "She's a nurse back home." In that moment, she was proud of her mom.

"Asante sana, asante sana!" The people at the clinic cried over and over again. They crowded around Hannah, stifling her. They reached out to touch her hair and the skin on her exposed forearms. She smiled through gritted teeth and froze.

Uncle Brian stepped in between Hannah and the crowd of sick patients. He leaned into her. "Karibu sana."

"What?" Hannah asked.

"Karibu sana. Means you're welcome. It will make them so happy if you say it to them." He stepped away and the crowd charged her again.

"Karibu sana," she winced and forced a smile.

Peanut Butter Crackers
and Protein Bars

Back at the Classic that evening, Hannah asked her mom about the peanut butter crackers and protein bars. "They need those at the clinic, Mom. You should have seen their reaction to the medicine you brought. It made me happy to give it to them. But I was so sad. And scared." Uncle Brian entered the room and Hannah quieted. She pushed the bed net to the side and sat down on the bed.

"What are you guys talking about?"

"Oh, nothing. It was really fun today."

"Hannah, come on. What were you talking about?" He insisted.

She looked down. Her lower lip quivered. "It's just . . ." Her mom walked over and sat down next to her. Hannah continued talking. "I don't want to upset you, Uncle Brian."

"Impossible! You could never upset me." He smiled. "Hannah, seriously, what's on your mind?" He pulled up the wooden chair and sat facing her.

"They have nothing!" She yelled and threw her arms down at her sides in exasperation. She walked over to the table and picked up a pack of peanut butter crackers. "And we brought these stupid snacks." She rubbed her stomach and talked in a baby voice. "In case I get an upset tums-tums while I'm here."

Uncle Brian laughed, got up and hugged her. "Well, your upset tums-tums needs to be taken care of, too."

She picked up a protein bar. "I feel like a complete loser. Can we take these to the clinic? Please?" She looked to her mom. "You haven't been feeling well, though. Is that okay with you?" Her mother nodded and Hannah smiled. It felt good to be nice to her mom.

"We sure can!" Brian added.

"Oh, but wait," her mom interrupted. *She really does ruin everything.* "What about nut allergies?" *Ah, that is a good point.*

Hannah reacted with instinct and read the label on the protein bar before hearing her uncle's answer. "Maybe we can still give them these," she muttered as she meticulously searched through the ingredients.

"No, that's okay," Uncle Brian said. "We can give it all to them. No one here—at least no one I've seen—has food allergies."

Hannah and her mom gasped. "No one?" Hannah asked, dumbfounded. "The number of kids at the nut-free table in the cafeteria at my school gets bigger and bigger each year. And I know there are some schools that have gone completely nut-free."

"Yeah, no one here has food allergies."

Hannah's eyes shifted and narrowed. *How is that possible? We're worried about what food to let in our schools and here they're worried about having food at all.* "I'm so glad food allergies are something they don't have to worry about here. That's incredible. I wish we didn't have to worry about them." She sat back down on the bed stunned by her revelation.

"You're right," Uncle Brian acknowledged. "We all have worries. Some of them are just very different worries." He picked up a pack of peanut butter crackers. "They'll love having this food, thank you. And speaking of things to take to the Clinic, I need to go to the Nakumatt tomorrow. Want to come with me? It's like Walmart! Remember the light bulbs?"

Hannah giggled. She recalled a Saturday night a few years earlier when Uncle Brian was between trips and had come over for a visit. Three light bulbs had blown in Hannah's house that evening, so Uncle Brian offered to run over to Walmart to get new ones. Hannah, who had just gotten home from a day at her friend's house, jumped in the car to go with him. As they drove off,

Uncle Brian looked at Hannah and said, "We're the coolest people I know, Hannah. Walmart on a Saturday night—WAHOO!" They laughed and made an evening of it playing on the Hippity Hops, checking out games on display, and racing down the aisles until the store manager began to eye them. "We should be totally embarrassed, but that was hilarious," Uncle Brian said, laughing as they walked out of the store. "At least we got the light bulbs!"

The next day, Jones drove Uncle Brian and Hannah to the Nakumatt while Meredith stayed at the Classic to help Grace prepare the meal for that evening. Hannah walked over to the bed nets. Some were labeled "treated". "What does it mean, treated versus untreated, Jones?"

"Is better treated," he answered. "Smelly," he scrunched his face and made a gagging noise, "but good for keep away mosquitoes!"

Hannah looked at the price tag as she put one in the cart. "Uncle Brian?" she leaned close and whispered. "They're only $7." She thought about all the babysitting money she had at home.

"I know," he said. He sounded discouraged.

"That's good, though, right? We can get a lot of them."

"They really do help prevent malaria. It's just that when we buy stuff and just give it to them, it makes them feel . . ." He hesitated. "I don't know, it just makes them feel like we're making donations. Or maybe it makes me feel bad that I get a salary for working to help and what I really should do is buy as many bed nets as I can. I'm never sure."

Hannah thought about what he was saying. She wanted to tell him about what her dad had said about poverty. And about her own worries.

Instead, all she could say was, "This isn't as fun as Walmart."

He perked up. "No!" he said. "I'm sorry, Hannah. I just get so caught up in it sometimes."

"That's not what I was thinking." She hung her shoulders and fought back tears. Jones walked to another aisle to give them privacy. "My dad said poverty will never end." She revealed as a tear escaped from her eye.

He sighed.

"I shouldn't have told you."

"No, no, that's okay, Hannah. I already knew that." He shrugged. "He's told me that himself many times."

"He has?" *What a jerk.*

"He is generous and donates a lot of money." He did not sound convincing.

She grunted. "Yeah, well, when I talked to him on the phone, he asked about the weather." She looked up at Brian, wiped the tear from her cheek and smiled. "I told him it was snowing."

They both laughed. She became serious again. "Uncle Brian?" He looked at her. "I'm not like my dad, but after seeing Sauri..." She sat down in the aisle, covered her head in her hands and cried. He sat down next to her.

"I know what you're saying. Believe me, I do. But you know, Hannah, you can never underestimate the power of progress. Little bits like your mom bringing medical supplies and you shopping for bed nets. And offering your peanut butter crackers and protein bars." Hannah sighed. "Sacrificing your own upset tums-tums and everything?" He jabbed her lightly and she started to laugh. "Let's get a bed net for Wilkister's family. You can give it to her as a thank you when she teaches you how to make the beaded bracelets. That's what's most valuable of all is getting to know the people—and then everything is possible."

"Do you really believe poverty will end?" She gulped.

"I do," he said. "And you know what else I believe?"

"What?"

He looked up and down the aisle where they were sitting on the floor. "That you and I cannot go shopping without making complete spectacles of ourselves!" Wiping the tears from her cheeks, Hannah giggled.

They bought a bed net, toiletries, and several jugs of bottled water. Hannah thought about her reusable water bottle at home—orange with a silver cap and a 26.2 sticker she had put on it to represent her goal of completing a marathon by the time she finished college. She could fill her bottle at water fountains at school, at the park, or from any one of her sinks at home. The only place to get drinkable water around there was the Nakumatt.

There was still no water at the Classic Guest House

when they returned that afternoon. It had been three days. That night, after another meal of fatty chicken and bitter kale she choked down with warm bottled water, she changed from her dirty clothes into her pajamas, which were just as dirty. She climbed under the bed net, held on to Beary, closed her eyes and, even though she knew she was happy to be there, she cried herself to sleep.

Mon Ami Club

"We'll go out to Sauri when I get back tomorrow," Uncle Brian announced over another breakfast of green oranges, stale bread, and hot tea.

"I thought we were going today," Hannah said. "We need to take the peanut butter crackers and protein bars. And the stuff we got yesterday. And when am I going to meet Wikis . . . Wisi . . ."

"Wilkister."

Hannah laughed. "Wilkister! Right. When can I meet her?"

"I'll take you as soon as I get back, I promise. But I just found out there's medicine in Nairobi that Dr. Omundo needs at the clinic."

"Can I go with you?" Her eyes sparkled.

"You can if you want to, but it's a long bus ride, Hannah, and Jones really wants to take you and your mom to the Mon Ami Club for lunch!"

Hannah cheered. Uncle Brian had told her about the Mon Ami Club, a local restaurant where they could order food from a menu. No more chicken and kale.

"Okay, but wait. Don't leave. Stay right here." She ran back up to her room and returned with two portable chargers. "Take these. Will they work with your phone?"

He inspected them. "They might. My phone is almost fully charged this time, but I'll take one just in case." He winked at her. "And Nairobi's the place to find an adapter if I need one."

Hannah smiled. "Take both of them. We haven't even gotten our phones to work yet." She thought of how she and her friends were attached to their phones 24/7 at home. She did not miss hers as much as she thought she would.

"Thanks, Hannah." She smiled. "And I should be back tomorrow. If not tomorrow, then early the next morning. Depends on the buses. There's a schedule, but you know how that goes." He laughed.

Realizing she was more rigid than she had thought, Hannah did not love not having a schedule. And she noticed people were not always watching the way they seemed to be at home. She remembered being on the boda-boda the other day. Feeling liberated and free, she had not been concerned about what people might think if she had fallen. No social media. No one commenting. She kind of liked it.

"So I'll be back in the next day or two, and then Hector will be back from Ethiopia next week, and then it will be Harvest Festival!"

Harvest Festival had become like a childhood bedtime story Hannah wanted read to her over and over. "Tell me about it again, Uncle Brian," she pleaded. "One more time."

"No one in Sauri has died because of hunger in a whole year, and we are going to celebrate!" He explained the community food program and the concept of taking what you need and leaving the rest for others. Of their corn and beans harvests, people had used what they needed and put the rest in the flour mill for others to have. "It's those little moments," he explained, "that build up to something big. And we are going to have fun at Harvest Festival!" He kissed Hannah on the head and got into the truck with Jones. "See you tomorrow!" He waved as they drove away.

"Or the next day!" Hannah called back.

He leaned his upper body out the window, looked back at her and waved. "Or the next day!"

Jones returned an hour later. On their drive to lunch, Hannah pointed out where she and Uncle Brian had taken boda-bodas. Jones parked the truck along a strip of parked trucks and cars, all fairly beaten up with dents and covered with a film of dirt. The town of Kisumu reminded Hannah of dust storms that enveloped the Wild West in history books she had read. She followed Jones out the driver's side, and as she leaned on to the door of the car to balance herself, the car door knocked into a small boy. "Oh my gosh, I'm sorry," she said to him as her feet touched the lumpy dirt ground. The boy was small, about forty pounds. He did not look like the kids she had seen in TV ads to help the hungry. His stomach was not distended with malnourishment. Instead he was bony and frail with a covering of dust so thick it lightened his dark African skin. In a swift movement, he got close to Hannah and said something she did not understand. Jones quickly moved toward him and responded in a serious, reprimanding tone. The boy ran off.

"He didn't do anything. I was the one who opened the car door right into him."

"He did that purpose, Hannah. He ask you for money," Jones explained. "I tell him just go home. Money is not help them." She thought back to what Uncle Brian had said in the Nakumatt.

They walked along a strip of small shops—an electronics store with massive TVs as deep as the screens were wide and remote controls the size of laptop computers and with just a few buttons. *How many people are buying TVs? There's hardly ever any electricity.* An internet café sold newspapers, served only water and juice, and had three boxy, dusty computers with thick, loose cords and a piece of worn white paper with black marker lettering 'sorry no internet' propped up in the window.

The ATM at the Barclay's Bank looked exactly like the ones at home. As her mom got out local currency, Hannah felt like she was jumping between two different lives: hers and this fictional one in Kenya. Nothing seemed real.

They stopped at a restaurant with a sign, 'Mon Ami Club'. The bar, barstools, tables and chairs were simple, carved from a light shade of wood with no texture or decoration. There was a clunky TV with fuzzy reception behind the bar showing a soccer game. A large cracked chalkboard displayed a menu of several options, including a veggie burger, broiled chicken, fried chicken, goat, and sides of kale, maize, or French fries. When the waiter came by, Hannah ordered a veggie burger, French fries and a Fanta orange soda. Her mom ordered broiled chicken with maize and a bottle of water, and Jones ordered broiled chicken with maize and kale. He drank tap.

Serving the people at the table next to theirs, a waiter stopped with a tray of food and a bottle with a label that caught Hannah's eye—Tusker, with the profile of an elephant.

"How long have you lived here, Jones?" she asked.

"I do not live Kisumu. I live Kitui."

"Kitui? Where's that?"

"About 400 kilometers east to Kisumu," he answered.

"A bus ride ten hour to here. I am here because I got job as driver of ICRAF. It is good job so I take home with money to Rebecca and Anthony, my wife and my son."

Jones explained that the land in Kitui is too dry to harvest and people are dying of hunger.

"Would you ever think about moving Rebecca and Anthony here, Jones?" Hannah's mom asked.

He shook his head. "Our family is Kitui. Brothers, sisters, and children—cousins to Anthony. Rebecca mum still alive and live with us," he said. "And she is old to move."

Hannah wondered Jones's age. He appeared young to have a child, especially one who was already six. "Do you mind if I ask how old you are, Jones?"

"I think..." Jones paused and took a drink. "About 25?" he said as if he were answering a trivia question and hoping to be right.

Hannah raised her left eyebrow and tilted her head to the right. "Do you know your birthday?"

"February."

She smiled.

"What about Anthony? When is his birthday?"

"Anthony born in October 28 and he six years old," he answered proudly.

The waiter put the lunches on the table. Hannah frowned at her plate of food. Instead of a bun, her veggie burger was held together with two slices of white bread.

She lifted the top slice and gagged. A lump of beans.

"Is okay the veggie burger?" Jones asked.

She nodded and smiled, trying not to laugh. She heard her mom stifle a giggle and knew they were thinking the same thing. *Funniest veggie burger ever.*

The lukewarm beans had made the bread soggy. She picked at the beans to be polite and devoured the thick cut French fries. The Fanta orange was very sweet, like having dessert with lunch.

The waiter put a check on their table. Hannah's mom promptly took the check and Jones thanked her. "Um, Jones?" her mom asked as she looked at the check. They had gotten Kenyan Shillings at the bank, so Hannah was not sure what the problem was. "Do you know about tipping? Back home, we give about 20% the cost of the meal to the waiter and it's called a tip. Do you do that here?"

"Please," he said, "leave what you can."

Leave what you can. Hannah thought back to what Brian had said about Harvest Festival and the community food program. No one in Sauri had died of hunger in a year because people had taken only what they needed.

The total cost of lunch was 880 KES, about $10. *Leave what you can.* The whole bill for three meals was less than what Hannah earned for an hour of babysitting at home. Her stomach ached with stress. And mushy beans.

Cell Phones and Snap What?

While walking back to the truck, Jones received a call from Patrick. He was at ICRAF and had called to tell Hannah and her mom that he had gotten their phones to work. Hannah was shocked. She leaned over to her mom. "How did Patrick figure it out?" she whispered.

"What do you mean?" her mom responded. "Why wouldn't he?"

Hannah did not want to answer out loud. *Because he is from Kisumu, Kenya. He doesn't have access to the Apple Genius Bar. And what does he know about technology anyway? If he could get them to work, why couldn't Uncle Brian? Why couldn't I?* Her eyebrows pointed inward and she let out a sigh.

They picked up the phones at ICRAF and thanked

Patrick. Hannah gave him an over-the-top hug to make up for the amount of guilt she felt for judging him.

With her cell phone back in her hand, Hannah felt a surge of energy like she had regained a superpower and had an immediate need to communicate with her friends back home. She looked at her phone screen. The icons for texting and Snapchatting had hollow circles in the upper corner where the number of messages should have been. Pressing each icon frantically, she could not get anything to happen. "Does Snapchat work here?" She asked, not looking up from her phone.

"Is Snap what?" Patrick responded.

Hannah looked up. Her mom was glued to her own screen.

"Snap is what?" Patrick asked again.

Hannah looked back to her mom who was still on her phone and sighed. *Get off your phone*, Mom. *Talk to people*, Mom. *Make eye contact*, Mom. *That's what you always say to me*. Responding to Patrick's question, Hannah said, "Oh, Snapchat is this thing to talk to your friends. Texting, too."

"Yes, yes," Jones said. He held up his cell phone. "Talk to your friends. With cell phone." Patrick smiled and nodded.

"Yes," Hannah acknowledged. "We can use our phones to call our friends, thanks to you." She smiled.

Looking up from her cell phone in defeat but smiling, Hannah's mom agreed. "Yes, we can use these to call home, thank you." Hannah rolled her eyes and sighed. *You probably only care because you want to text Dad instead of having to talk to him.*

"We can still take pictures, though!" Hannah remembered. She huddled with Patrick and Jones and took a selfie. She showed them. "It's called a selfie," she explained. "You take pictures of yourself and your friends." Jones and Patrick laughed. Hannah looked at the picture. She was so dirty. *Maybe it's a good thing I can't Snapchat.*

When Jones, Hannah and her mom pulled into the Classic that evening, Grace and Ash were waiting for them out front, Grace with her usual enormous smile, Ash sitting to her left, wagging his tail. With a big, open-mouthed grin, Grace extended her arms toward the guesthouse as if there were a big surprise inside. Hannah knew *exactly* what she meant.

Without saying a word, she ran up the stairs and through the door to her room and into the bathroom. She took in a deep breath and held it as she turned the shower faucet. Water! So much of it! She took her clothes off, left them in a heap, and put her glasses on the side of the sink. Without hesitation, she jumped in. She let out a squeal and ran back out on to her pile of dirty clothes. Shivering, she got back in and fought through the icy coldness of the water, not wanting to take it for granted. She looked down at herself. She had not realized just how thick a layer of dirt had enveloped her body and was afraid the mud would clog the drain, but she did not worry too long about it. The feeling of being clean overtook her. She let the water rush over her filthy face. She reached over and grabbed a bar of soap they had bought at the Nakumatt. The lather and the suds felt so good, so fresh, so clean. She stepped away from the mud that continued to gather along the drain. She thought of saving water for her mom to shower, for the others to have a shower, but she could not bring herself to turn the knob.

"Hannah?" she heard her mom call from the room. "Dad's on the phone. He wants to talk with you."

Hannah grabbed a towel—small and ratty but clean—and covered herself, then took the phone from her mom. Her mom, handing the phone to Hannah, burst out laughing at Hannah's delighted expression.

"Hey, Dad."

"Hi, Han. How are things out there?"

"Good! We got stuff at the Nakumatt to take out to Sauri when Uncle Brian gets back tomorrow."

Her dad interrupted. "Wait, Uncle Brian's not with you?"

"He went to Nairobi for the day to get medicine. They can't ship it." She put her free hand up in the air and gestured as if he could see her as she explained. "There are no post offices."

"Can you put Mom back on the phone, please, Hannah? Right now." His voice was stern.

"Wait, Dad." She pleaded.

"I just don't want you and Mom left all alone there." The way he said 'there' was offensive. "It's time for both of you to come home."

"No!" She snapped. "They're taking such good care of us here. Grace, Jones, Patrick, and even Hector before he left for Ethiopia yesterday. All of Uncle Brian's friends, they . . ."

"I know, Hannah." He interrupted. "Brian has lots of friends. That's great." His sarcasm was palpable.

"It's been four days!" she yelled. She looked around and quieted her voice. "It's only been four days, Dad. We're staying for three weeks. Uncle Brian is going to be back tomorrow and we're going out to Sauri again. As I said before..." Her words slowed and she felt her tone becoming obnoxious, but she could not stop it. "We're taking food and medicine out to the Sauri Clinic, and there's a girl out there Uncle Brian wants me to meet. We're going to make bracelets together. Her name is Wikis... Wilkie... Well, it starts with a W, and I can't wait to meet her." She leaned out of the room and called to her mom to come get the phone. As she reached down the stairs to hand it to her, she put the phone back up to her ear. "And we're not coming home yet." She went to hand the phone to her mom and pulled it back again. "Give Livvy a kiss for me and I love you," she muttered all in one breath and handed the phone to her mom.

She went back to the bathroom to brush her clean hair and wash her face one more time. She was not going to let anything ruin her happy feeling. She had waited four days for water. Clean, running water.

If We Have It,
Shouldn't Everyone Have It?

The following morning, Hannah woke up before her mom. Still giddy with cleanliness, she quietly climbed out of bed and then leaned back in to prop Beary up on her pillow. Giggling at the sight of Beary sleeping next to her mom under the bed net, Hannah walked into the bathroom, took in a breath, and turned the faucet knob. *Water two days in a row!* She washed her face and used bottled water to brush her teeth.

After closing the door to her room behind her, Hannah walked downstairs. She glared up at the sun shining an intense light over her and checked her cell phone. 5:30 a.m. The tap-tap sound of four little paws approaching made her smile. "Ash," she whispered. "We're the only ones up." She took a picture of the two of them. *I'll show this to Livvy as soon as I get home.* She giggled.

She sat down at the picnic table and took a swig from her water bottle. *What I'd give for an ice cube.* She looked at the picture of Ash and her. *Something about me looks different. And it's not the dirty clothes.* Out of the corner of her eye, she saw a newspaper sticking out from underneath the table. *News. I haven't even thought about what's going on. My whole world has been western Kenya.*

She leaned down and picked up the paper. She thought of newspaper delivery kids on bikes at home and wondered if the kids here delivered the newspaper on boda-bodas. Placing the newspaper on the table, she flipped through it. Political upheaval nationally. Weather affecting the crops locally. She turned the page. An oil tanker overturned just outside Kisumu, causing a major fire. She pushed her glasses up on her nose between her eyes and looked more closely at the picture.

She grabbed her cell phone and scrolled the contacts to call her uncle. *It's kind of early to call, but he won't care. He's probably on his way home anyway, and he won't be able to sleep on the bus. Not with all the bumpy roads.* It was ringing. Letting out a sigh of relief, she thought of what she'd say first. *There was an accident in the newspaper and it made me nervous. I just want you to come home.* She smiled at her thought of referring to Kisumu as home. They had not even been there a week, but she loved the people. She got his voicemail. "Hi Uncle Brian. I just miss you. Call me and let me know when you'll be back, okay? It's just that I miss you. Oh wait, I said that already." She laughed into the phone, momentarily forgetting her nervousness. "I love you. Can't wait to see you! Bye."

Hustling upstairs, she went to wake her mom. "Mom?" She tugged at the bed net. Her mom stirred.

"I don't feel great, Hannah."

"You're just nervous, Mom." She dismissed her complaint. "And now I am, too. Uncle Brian isn't answering his phone."

Her mom sat up in bed and moved the bed net aside. "Why did you call him?" She rubbed her eyes, picked up her phone and looked at the screen. "What time is it?"

Hannah shrugged. "You don't understand, Mom. A truck overturned and caused a fire!"

She gasped and stood up. "Where?"

"I don't know. Somewhere. Somewhere in Kenya. It was in the paper."

"Hannah." Her mom sat back down on the bed. "Kenya is a big country. And that was a truck, not a bus." Patting the mattress for Hannah to sit down next to her, she pulled the bed net back farther to make room. Hannah sat and picked Beary up from the pillow. "You can't worry so much." Her mom laughed softly. "Or you'll end up like me."

Hannah nestled into her mom. "That wouldn't be so

bad."

Ash raced into the room with Grace calling after him. "Ash! No! Come!" She stopped at the entrance and called from outside the open door, "I so sorry."

Amused, Hannah's mom invited her in. "We don't mind," she insisted. Letting out an aching groan as she leaned over to pet Ash, she said, "We have a dog at home."

Grace came in and picked Ash up. "I know." She smiled. "Is Livvy. Brian tell me. She not good at listening either."

Laughing, Hannah and her mom agreed. "No, she is not. But we still love her." Hannah took Ash from Grace and scratched behind his ears. "And we love you."

"We go to market today, is good?" Grace asked.

"Sure!" Hannah said. "Can we take boda-bodas?"

Grace nodded.

"That sounds perfect, Grace, thank you. We'll be downstairs in just a few minutes." Hannah's mom coughed faintly.

She nodded again. "Okay, Ash. We go downstairs now. You see Hannah again, I promise." Hannah kissed Ash on the head and put him down. He trotted out the door alongside Grace, shoulders arched back, nose pointed in the air, tail wagging.

As soon as Grace had started down the stairs, Hannah's mom leaned back into the bed. "Hannah?" she asked. "Is it okay if I rest while you and Grace go to the market? You won't be gone too long and I'll be better by the time you get back and by then Uncle Brian should be home." Hannah smiled. *You said home too.* "Is that okay? I'm sorry." Her head had already hit the pillow.

Hannah climbed in the bed and put Beary back on the pillow next to her mom. "Don't be sorry. And Beary will keep you company."

Her mom laughed. "Thanks, Beary." She patted him on the head and laid her head back on the pillow.

Feeling her own stomach start to ache, Hannah thought about all the medicine they had taken before they left for Kenya. Preventative medicine meant to protect them from sickness. *Maybe that's what's making Mom sick.* Gazing out the window, she remembered years ago when Uncle Brian had visited before going to Africa for the first time.

"I made you chocolate chip cookies, Uncle Brian, your favorite!"

"Thanks, Hannah. I'm going to have one later, though, all right?" he said, shifting from his left side to his right on the couch under a blanket. "I'm a little envious of Liv right now." They looked at Livvy, belly-up and snoring, on the far end of the couch.

"Want a pillow?" she asked.

Smiling, he said, "I already have one!" He leaned up. She saw Beary against the cushion behind him and laughed.

"Let Uncle Brian rest, Hannah," her dad called from the kitchen.

"No, no, no," insisted her weak uncle. "Please stay. I can't possibly sleep anymore." Using his elbow to prop himself up, he called back to her dad. "I want her to stay, Dan."

"What's the matter anyway?" Hannah asked.

"Well, you know I am going to be doing some work in parts of Africa, right? I went to the travel clinic today and got some shots—yellow fever, hepatitis A and B, meningitis, typhoid. Ugh, that yellow fever one was bad. They have to refrigerate it, I'm not sure why, but that one was the worst. Look." He pointed to his upper left arm. "It left a huge bruise! Nasty, huh?"

"Yeah, I guess," Hannah answered, biting her lower lip. "Are you done with the shots?"

"I am," he said. "I just need to take pills to prevent malaria."

"Malaria. That's the mosquitoes one."

He nodded.

Hannah looked at her uncle, feverish, sore and uncomfortable. The bruise on his arm looked really painful. "I'm sorry you're sick, and not just because I want to hang out. I am really sorry you're not feeling well."

"Aw, thanks, Hannah. Me, too. This is going to sound weird, but I'm actually the lucky one right now. First of all, I have you baking me your awesome chocolate chip cookies."

She smiled.

"And I get to have these shots."

Tilting her head to the side and scrunching her nose, she asked, "How is that lucky?"

"When I get to Africa, I won't have to worry about getting sick because these shots are preventing me from getting the actual diseases. People over there aren't so lucky. There aren't the shots and pills there to prevent them from getting sick. And on top of that, there isn't medicine to help cure them or even make them more comfortable. That's the real tragedy—that the medicine exists, but they don't have it."

"Why don't we just send them medicine? I mean, if we have it, shouldn't everyone have it?" Hannah asked.

"Yes," he said. Lifting his aching body, he sat up next to her. "Everyone should have it. But they don't."

She remembered his words so clearly. *Everyone should have it. But they don't.* With tears in her eyes, she looked at her mom under the bed net. Her mom had always taken care of her when she was sick, and not just because she was a good nurse. Because she was a great mom. Searching her mind for what she could do, she asked, "Mom? Want some of the peanut butter crackers? Do you think the Nakumatt has ginger ale?"

Without lifting her head, her mom said, "Thank you, Hannah. I'm fine. Really. I just need some rest."

"Do you think it's all the medicine we took?"

She opened her eyes and leaned up in bed. "Really, I'm fine. Thank you for caring so much, Hannah." She smiled.

"Thank me so much for caring?" She put her hands on her hips. "Of course I care!" She insisted. "I love you, Mom."

Her mom smiled as she put her head back down. "I know you do, Hannah. I love you, too." It was as though she was already half asleep. "Go have fun with Grace and I'll be downstairs when you get back."

Hannah pulled the bed net back and gave her mom a kiss on the head. She leaned in further and kissed Beary, too. "Take care of her," she whispered and walked out the door.

Africa Time, Errands, and Dad

Without a schedule, Hannah was early for everything. She did not ease into the idea of Africa time. Instead, she became even more aware of time. And how long they had been away, which seemed a lot longer than five days. She waited with Ash for Grace to get ready to go to the market.

"Is all good," Grace said. "I just prepare for dinner tonight. Special treat for you. And Brian come home." Smiling, she patted Ash on the head and took Hannah's arm. "Is good we take boda-boda?"

"Yes!" Hannah skipped along beside Grace. Ash whimpered. "We'll be right back, Ash. Don't you worry!" She blew him a kiss and continued walking out of the Classic Guest House.

Hannah felt free. Always having Jones to drive her,

she had gotten used to having him around. It was definitely a little different with a female chaperone than a male—she liked the idea of a day out with just the ladies.

They took boda-bodas to town. Realizing she forgot to get money from her mom, Hannah called out to Grace, who was on a bike just ahead of her. Grace looked back over her shoulder and said, "Hannah, is okay. I pay for you is good." When they arrived, Hannah watched Grace pay the riders. Nervously snapping together the nails of her thumb and middle finger, Hannah bit her lower lip and was mad at her mom for not remembering to give her money.

"Hannah?"

She looked up. Grace had walked ahead and was waiting for her.

"Come, Hannah. I need get maize for dinner and I get you beads for make bracelets with Wilkister. Brian ask me."

Hannah raced up ahead. "You know Wilkister?"

"I never meet Wilkister but Brian tell me she is good girl." Grace put her arm around Hannah as they walked. "And you are!"

They bought six ears of corn. "I can husk them," Hannah offered. And they walked further into the market where there were baskets of beads. Hannah's eyes widened. She frowned when she thought again about money. "I don't have any money, Grace. Can I pay you back when we get home?" *Home.*

Grace laughed. "No, no, Hannah. I buy for you. Is no problem." She leaned into her. "But you make me a bracelet, okay?"

"Yes!"

Together, they picked out assorted beads, wire, and clasps. Hannah loved running her fingers through the smooth beads. "Thank you, Grace."

When they arrived back at the Classic, Hannah's mom raced out to meet them in the gravel driveway with her arm reaching out toward Hannah. "Dad's on the phone." *He probably only called two minutes ago, and already she wants to pass him off.*

Hannah took the phone from her mom. "Hi, Dad," she said. "Isn't it really early? What are you doing up?"

"Last night were the 4th of July fireworks. Liv is still a complete wreck!"

"Oh, no. I completely forgot about the 4th of July. The fireworks were that bad?"

"She's still shaking. And she was up most of the night."

"Oh, that's so sad. Give her a kiss for me. And a hug." She looked down at Ash, who wagged his tail, waiting for a pet. She scratched behind his ears. *I wonder if you'd be afraid of the fireworks.*

"Done," he said. "So, how are things?"

"Good," she answered. "Uncle Brian should be back soon. Grace is making a special dinner."

"What's she making?"

"I don't know." She walked farther down the driveway away from where anyone could hear her and whispered, "And I really don't care as long as it's not chicken and kale."

He laughed. "Well," he said. "I promise to have a cheese pizza ready for you when you get back." *It's like he's bribing me to come home. At least he's not asking about the weather.* She smiled. And salivated.

"Deal," she said. "Oh, and we got beads at the market today. I am going to make bracelets with Wilkister when we go out to Sauri tomorrow."

"Brian will definitely be back tonight?"

"I hope so. If not tonight, he'll be here by tomorrow morning. You know, the bus schedule." *He doesn't know.*

"Okay, well, I'll call again tomorrow. Have a good rest of the day, Hannah."

"Thanks, Dad. You, too."

"Oh, and Hannah?"

"Yeah?"

"Enjoy your special meal tonight. I bet it's going to be great." Tears welled up in Hannah's eyes. *He's trying. He really is. So is Mom. I need to give them both a break.*

"Thanks, Dad. I love you."

"Love you, too. Bye."

"Bye."

Hannah held the phone up to her chest, rested her chin down over it, and stared down at the gravel. *I wish you were here, Dad.*

Surprise Meal

"Grace has a surprise dinner for us tonight. I am not sure what it is—she wouldn't tell me—but I have a feeling it's not chicken and kale." Her mom said when Hannah got back upstairs.

Hannah nodded and smiled, trying to share in her mom's enthusiasm and the excitement of Grace's surprise meal, but she could not stop thinking about her dad. And Uncle Brian had not gotten back yet. And there was no more running water. Grabbing a bottle of water, Hannah said, "I promised I'd husk the corn." She felt the sides of the water bottle. Even the plastic was a little warm. She looked up at her mom, who was sitting on the bed. "Are you feeling better?"

Her mom got up and walked with her. "It seems to

come and go." *It's called nerves.* "But yes, I feel better now, thanks."

"Cow's meat!" Grace exclaimed over a big pot of boiling water. "Is special treat for my special friends."

Ooooh, Hannah thought. *Steak. Yum!* She licked her lips.

"Hannah, maize is outside on table. You will husk for me?" Hannah nodded. She and her mom went outside. Hannah husked the corn while her mom placed the plastic red-and-white checked tablecloth over the wooden picnic table. Taking plates and utensils that Grace had cleaned in boiling water, Hannah's mom set the table and put a pile of paper napkins in the center. Hannah looked for something to put on the napkins to keep them from blowing away and then laughed. *Not necessary.* She finished husking the corn and took it to Grace.

Grace walked out with the pot. Holding it with a tan-and-pink floral potholder, she put it down on another potholder that she had tossed onto the table. She put meat on each person's plate.

Hannah tried to disguise her disappointment. There was more bone than meat. Big bones. Thick bones. As she investigated more closely, she saw there was hardly any meat at all. It was mostly fat. *Cow's meat is not steak.* She wished for chicken and kale.

"Thank you, Grace. Asante sana," she said and sat down at the table. Smiling, Grace put corn on each person's plate. A place had been set for Uncle Brian in case he came back while they were eating.

They held hands and Grace said a prayer, as she did before every meal. The prayer was said in Swahili, so she explained that she had thanked God for His kindness and warmth, and for this beautiful meal. *Beautiful meal?* Luckily there was corn. Hannah would fill up on that. But she had to eat the meat. And she could not hide it in the corn the way she used to hide food she did not want to eat when she was little. Taking a big bite of corn and a small bite of cow's meat, she hoped to hide the taste. It worked— sort of. She continued eating until she had cleared her plate, everything except the bones, and thanked Grace for the wonderful surprise.

Back upstairs, she wanted to splash water on her sweaty face, but there was still no water. She felt kale stuck in her teeth. Squeezing toothpaste onto her dirty index finger, she rubbed it across her top and bottom teeth and rinsed with a swig of warm bottled water. She poured more of the bottled water on a towel and pressed it against her hot, filthy face. She heard a "tsssss" hiss like a snake when the cloth touched her stinging eyes. As she removed it from her face, she looked at it caked with dirt. She changed into a grey t-shirt and light blue pajama bottoms, climbed under the insecticide treated bed net into bed and curled up with Beary while her mom used the bathroom.

"That was gross, Mom," Hannah whispered as her

mom crawled into bed beside her. "Really gross." She moaned and scrunched her knees into her chest. "I don't feel so good."

Her mom got out of bed and picked up a pack of peanut butter crackers on the dresser. "Here." She tossed them to Hannah. "These will settle your stomach."

Hannah sat up, opened the pack, and popped one into her mouth. Savoring the peanut butter, she could taste each individual crystal of salt on the crackers. She closed her eyes as she chewed and could even hear herself making an "Mmmmm" sound. She opened her eyes and gasped as though she had been woken up from a dream. When she gasped, she choked on a piece of cracker and started to cough. Pushing away the bed net, she grabbed a water bottle at the side of the bed.

"What's wrong, Hannah? Are you okay?"

Chugging the water, Hannah's breathing became regular again. And she started to cry.

"What is it?" Her mom raised her eyebrows and rubbed Hannah's arm. "What happened?"

Hannah wrapped the remaining crackers in the packaging and handed them back to her mom. "I pictured the people at the clinic in Sauri. And they looked so hungry. And sad. And scared… And sick. They need these crackers, not me."

Her mom continued rubbing Hannah's arm. "I know," she said gently.

CHAPTER 15

Hannah pulled away. "You don't know, Mom!" She gritted her teeth. "You weren't there, remember? You stayed back just like you did today. You don't know." She cried harder but kept her voice quiet. "And I'm calling her special dinner gross and she worked so hard on it. And probably spent a lot of money, too. You forgot to give me money today and she had to pay for everything!"

Her mom bit her fingernails. "Oh, I did forget to give you money." She got money out of her backpack and put some in Hannah's little blue purse with a pink elephant on it. "You'll have this for next time. I'm sorry."

Taking another gulp of water, Hannah lay back down on the bed. Not looking at her mom, she apologized. "It's not your fault. I'm just tired." *The excuse of being tired. We now have that in common.* "I'll be better when Uncle Brian gets back."

Jones Knows

Ash's barking startled Hannah out of a deep sleep. Propping herself up with her elbow, she wiped the drool from the side of her mouth. Her neck and upper back ached. She rubbed her crusty eyes. The blue elastic that held her hair in a ponytail had fallen out. Reaching through the bed net to her backpack, she grabbed another one and tied her hair back in a disheveled heap. She rubbed her tired eyes and put on her glasses. Feeling bloated and gross, she nudged her mom.

"Uncle Brian must be back!" She raced into the bathroom and turned the faucet. Nothing. She squeezed some toothpaste into her mouth, took a swig of warm bottled water, swished it around and spit it out in the sink. *Good enough.* She ran downstairs.

"Ash! Where are you?" Ash raced toward her and jumped up. She caught him and held him in her arms. Grace walked in behind him.

"Hi, Grace. Is Uncle Brian home?"

"Hi sweetie pie. You are so good." She looked around. "No, no, I do not see Brian. I thought he back when I hear Ash bark."

"Me, too." Hannah sat down at the table.

"You want hot tea? An orange?"

"Yes, please." Hannah answered. *What I'd give for an iced tea. With lemon. And an orange that's not green.*

The morning newspaper was on the table, still folded. Hannah opened it and read the cover story headline. "Bus From Nairobi to Kisumu Crashes, Killing All Passengers and Driver." She inhaled, put the newspaper up close to her face, and looked at the black and white picture. Eight large wheels intact over a smashed bus in a jagged gray landscape with ominous flames and deep black smoke wafting up into the sky above it. She could not see any people. Exhaling, she quickly scanned the article for information about the bus—where it originated, what time it left Nairobi. There were no specifics.

She screamed. "Grace! Mom!" Grace came running. She handed her the paper and ran past her and up the stairs. "Mom!" She yelled.

At the top of the stairs, she grabbed her cell phone from her pocket and scrolled through the contacts. Her thumb froze on Uncle Brian. She pressed down. It went right into voicemail. *Why didn't he use the portable charger?* She slammed her phone on the banister. "Where is he?" She cried and raced into her room.

"Mom! Wake up, Mom!" She tugged at the bed net.

Seeming almost translucent, her mom's skin glistened with beads of sweat. Hannah watched as her mom sat up. She seemed unaware of her surroundings. "Hannah? What time is it?"

"Uncle Brian's not back." She sniffed. "And a bus to Nairobi flipped and killed everyone on it." Wiping the tears from her face, she whispered the words, not wanting to speak them aloud. "No one has heard from Uncle Brian since he left."

Her mom pushed the bed net aside and stood up. She took a step back and held the side of her forehead. Beary fell from the pillow onto the mattress. Shoulders back, straight as a pin—resembling the Pointer dog from the airport—her mom walked downstairs still in her nightgown. Taking several quick steps to catch up with her mom, Hannah grabbed her by the arm and followed her. She nestled her head into her mom's shoulder as they walked.

When they got downstairs, they saw Grace holding her head in her palms. Keeping her face shielded, she moved her hands away from her mouth to speak. "Jones come over. He know."

"He knows what?" Hannah's mom asked. She took a deep breath in. Hannah had not stopped crying.

Grace remained silent with her hands over her face.

Hannah's mom exhaled. "Grace!" she snapped. "Jones knows what?"

Grace moved her hands from the front of her face to its sides. She pressed them hard against her cheeks, revealing the tears in her eyes. "He know Brian was on that bus."

Shattered

Uncle Brian had called Jones and asked him to pick him up at the bus station. That was how he knew. Brian had been on the bus that flipped, killing all 33 passengers plus the driver. Patrick had called the bus station to verify the names of the passengers. It was certain. Uncle Brian was dead.

With her fingers pressing against her temples and her thumbs pushed into her cheeks, Hannah went through the timing minute by minute. *Did he get my message? Does he know I loved him?* She sobbed. *Not loved him. Love him. Does he know I love him? Of course he does. But did he get my message before… he got on the bus? He must have. Right?* She gasped when she remembered she wanted to go with him. *I should have been on that bus.* She cried harder. *I wish I had been.*

She looked around the table—her mom, Grace, Jones, and Patrick—all staring in different random directions. Stunned.

"We need to call Dad," Hannah's mom said stoically. Hannah looked up at her mom. *This could not possibly be code for "you need to call Dad." No way. Not now.* Her mom took her cell phone and walked away. *Thank goodness. But I still want to talk to him.* Following her mom around the corner of the Classic Guest House, Hannah listened in on the conversation.

For as much as her mom drove her crazy and as often as her parents fought, Hannah had rarely seen her mom cry. And she was sobbing. "I'm so sorry." Hannah heard her say over and over. Then she said, "We'll be home in less than two weeks." *What?* Hannah heard her dad's voice utter the same word through the phone and from ten feet away where she was standing.

Her mom explained that they had to stay to continue the work in Sauri and to be there for Harvest Festival. *Continue the work in Sauri? That's a joke! You haven't done anything. Neither have I. Continue the work?* Unable to listen any longer, with her feet planted firmly on the ground, she made two fists and screamed. "Are you kidding me? Continue the work? What work? We haven't done anything. We've only been out to Sauri one day. And Grace, Jones, and Patrick have spent the whole time taking care of us!"

Her mom shushed her. "Hannah, let me talk to Dad and you and I can talk later."

"No!" She yelled. She grabbed the phone from her mom. "Dad? I want to come home!" she wailed.

"Of course, Sweetie. You come home. Leave Mom there."

"Leave Mom here? What are you talking about? You need to come get us."

"I can't leave work, Hannah. But I'll arrange for a ticket home for you." He sounded so calm. And she was disgusted. "You can get to the airport and I'll text you with what flight you're on."

She pressed the phone against her face. "Text! Doesn't! Work!" She threw it across the gravel driveway. It shattered to pieces.

She ran upstairs and slammed the door to her room. Pulling the bed net away, she crawled into bed and hugged Beary. She cried herself to sleep.

If We Leave Now

"Hannah? Sweetie? Do you want something to eat? Something to drink? Jones said he could drive us to the Nakumatt. Or he could pick something up for us if we tell him what we want." Her mom's gentle voice made her cringe.

Hannah sat up in bed and put Beary in her lap. She gazed upward and noticed something mystical about the inside of the bed net. Feeling like she was in a trance, she robotically picked up her cell phone. Three missed calls from her dad.

"Han?" Her mom pulled against the opening of the bed net and sat down. "I owe you an apology."

"Yes, you do!" Hannah screamed as she came back to reality. "And continue the work here? Are you kidding me?

What work? We haven't done one thing to help anyone. Everyone here has been taking care of us. Taking care of you." She was disgusted. "And we are not staying here. I don't want to be here without Uncle Brian." She cried. *I don't want to be anywhere without Uncle Brian.*

"Would you please let me apologize?"

Hannah did not budge. *How many tears can a person cry? Must be billions. Trillions.*

Her mom moved closer to her. "I'm sorry that I made a decision for the two of us without talking to you first. And I'm sorry I said we needed to continue the work here. That's not what I meant. We take care of each other. You and me. Grace, Patrick, Jones. The people out in Sauri. We all take care of each other. You are so right about that. And that's what I meant to say. That's what I should have said."

Hannah wiped the tears from her cheeks and looked up at her mom.

"Brian was so excited for us to celebrate Harvest Festival, and I think we should stay for it. I think I should still help in the clinic. I think you should still meet Wilkister and make bracelets. I think we should stay, Hannah. I really do."

Hannah thought about it. She handed her phone to her mom. "Can you call Dad back? I don't want to talk to him." Her mom nodded.

"If we leave now..." Starting to cry, her mom continued talking. "If we leave now, we will remember

Brian dying. But if we leave after Harvest Festival and spending more time here, we'll also get to have the memory of all the happiness he brought to all of us. That's what we'll remember."

Holding Beary in one arm, Hannah hugged her mom with the other. "That's what I want to remember." She sniffled. "That's what I want to remember."

Room in Our Hearts

Hannah ran her fingers across the front seat of the truck as she slid across to make room for her mom, Patrick, and Jones. Her head felt heavy and it fell forward between her slouched shoulders. Even sitting in the car made her sad.

Jones patted her on the knee before he started the engine. No one said a word. Grace called out to them, "I have dinner ready when you get back." It took all Hannah had in her to lift her arm and wave bye to Grace.

Everything felt heavy. And there seemed to be a cloud of dust around her. She looked around. There was. But it felt different than it had. No longer the dust in the rural air, it had become weighted and blurry. Nothing made any sense. She heard her mom's voice with words here and there, but was not connecting them. She did not need to. She knew the plan. Patrick had called ahead to Dr. Omundo to tell him about Uncle Brian's death. He was going with Hannah and her mom to the clinic for the day. Jones would go to the school and alert the Head Teacher, Anne Odhiambo. Jones had invited Hannah to go with him, but she had insisted on staying with her mom. Reminding her about meeting Wilkister, Hannah had told him, "I don't want to meet her anymore. I just want to stay with my mom."

The bumpy ride out to Sauri bothered her less that morning. The heaviness in her body seemed to ground her. And not quite able to lift her head, her gaze remained at dashboard level making the jagged roads less jarring. When they arrived in Sauri, Hannah slumped out of the car and rested her tired body up against her mom. The intense heat of the sun no longer seemed to affect her. She wished she were a toddler again so she could put her arms in the air for her mom to pick her up and hold her.

When they arrived at the clinic, Dr. Omundo shook their hands and expressed his condolences. Her mom's inner nurse took over and she started treating the patients. *It's like his death is fueling her. My tank is empty.*

"I'll check back in with you, Hannah. I just need to . . ." Her voice trailed off as she tended to the first person in line, a young mother with her baby who was weak or unconscious. Hannah looked at the line of people waiting, endless amounts of sick people needing assistance. She recognized one man who had been there when she had gone to the clinic with Uncle Brian. It had been only five days. Irritated, rashy skin, sunken, yellowed eyes, incessant cough, she wondered what he had—and whether it was contagious. She walked outside, sat on the dry ground with the chickens and waited.

"Jambo! Allo? Jambo! You are Hannah?" She pronounced Hannah with the emphasis on NAH. Hah-NAH. "I am Wilkister."

"Hi," Hannah said and stood up. The chickens dispersed around her.

Wilkister rushed to her, put her forehead on Hannah's shoulder and hugged her at the waist. "My teacher tell me about Brian. I so sad." She cried.

Hannah kept her arms straight to her sides and looked around. Seeing nothing over Wilkister's shoulders but brown landscape, she asked, "Where did you come from?"

Wilkister took a step back from Hannah. She wiped her tears. "I come from school. You want come to school?"

Hannah snarled her upper lip. "Why would I want to go to school with you?" Emphasizing the word "you", she heard herself sounding like the mean girls at her school. Through squinted eyes, she looked at Wilkister's purple dress, weathered, dusty and torn at the bottom and on the side. Her feet were bare.

Sniffing and catching her breath, Wilkister said, "I just . . . I just want see you." She paused. "Brian say we will be friends."

Hannah responded, monotone. "I have beads for you. Oh, and I have a bed net for your family. It's from my Uncle Brian. I'll bring them out to you tomorrow."

Wilkister smiled. "Thank you." Wrinkles formed in her forehead as she shyly looked up at Hannah. "You want make bracelets together?" She looked back down.

Hannah shook her head. "I don't think so. But I'll bring the beads out tomorrow. Jones can take them to school for you." Hearing herself sound like a jerk, she was disgusted. But she could not help it.

Putting her hands on her hips, Wilkister snapped back. "I have my own beads." She ran off.

Hannah sat back down with the chickens, who walked away clucking. *Even the chickens don't want to be with me.*

Back at the Classic that night, Hannah sat by herself at the picnic table. Her mom had gone upstairs to rest. Grace prepared dinner, Ash by her side.

A splinter in the bench caught on her skirt. As she brushed it aside, it ripped a tiny bit and she got a splinter on the side of her pinky. She picked at it to get it out.

"Hannah? Sweetie pie. You are okay?" Grace walked out and sat down next to her. Ash jumped up onto the bench and took a spot between them.

Hannah looked up and then at her finger. "Yes, I'm okay. I just have this splinter. I'll be able to get it."

Grace took her hand. "Let me see." Using her fingernail, she scratched at it lightly over and again in the same direction until she got it out. She was a bit triumphant, which made Hannah smile for the first time in two days.

"Hannah, you are so good." She got up to check on dinner.

Hannah looked down and tears welled up. Her smiling lips started to quiver. "No, I'm not," she whispered.

Grace stopped and turned around back toward Hannah. "Is what you say?"

"I'm not good," she shook her head and cried softly.

Grace looked over toward the kitchen and nervously bit her upper lip. Racing into the kitchen to stir the pot of boiling water and chicken, she came right back and sat down with her hip touching Hannah's. She rubbed Hannah's back and said, "You are so good. Why you say you're not?"

"I was so mean to Wilkister!" she blurted out.

"Ah, you meet Wilkister today!" Grace said. "But why you were mean? What happen?"

Hannah cried. "I was so mad she was so upset about my Uncle Brian. He's *my* uncle! And we were supposed to hang out with him together, not just me and her." She breathed in unsteadily. Her voice softened. "I was mad that she got to spend so much time with him." She flopped her body into Grace's and cried harder. "I want more time with him!" she wailed.

Grace held her for a long time. Ash pawed at Hannah's skirt and she picked him up. The three of them sat in silence for a while.

"Brian have enough room in his heart for everyone," Grace said. Hannah sat up, holding Ash with one arm and wiping her tears away with her other.

"What do you mean?"

"Brian have enough room in his heart for everyone," she repeated. "Yes, he love Wilkister, he love her family, he love me, he love all his friends here, he love your parents. He love *you*." She emphasized "you" the same way Hannah had in her conversation with Wilkister. Only this emphasis was so kind. Hannah's had been so mean. "You are like Brian, Hannah. You have room in your heart."

"Room in my heart for everyone," Hannah whispered. Looking around her and out to the horizon, she smiled and hugged Grace. "Thank you, Grace!" As she raced up the stairs, she called back. "And *you* are so good!" She emphasized "you".

A Second Chance with Wilkister

The following morning, Hannah was the first one downstairs. Balancing the bag of beads, wire and clasps in one hand and the bed net in the other, she wobbled to the truck. Jones saw her struggling and ran from the picnic table to help her. "What you have here?" He took the bag of beads from her, put them on the seat and moved the bed net into the back of the truck.

"I forgot the peanut butter crackers! Hang on." She dashed back upstairs. Her mom was walking out the door. "I forgot the peanut butter crackers," she repeated.

Her mom patted her purse. "I have everything."

Hannah smiled.

"I talked to Dad last night, Han."

Her smile disappeared.

"You're going to have to call him when we get back tonight, okay?"

Hannah nodded.

"He's not mad. It's just that he wants us to come home. But he knows we're staying for Harvest Festival. He'll be at the airport to pick us up when we get back."

She shrugged her shoulders. "Okay, I'll call him when we get back."

Hannah held the beads in her lap on the drive to Sauri. She held onto her mom with her other arm and stared out the dusty windshield. Jones drove. Patrick had gone to the site of the bus accident and was taking care of all the arrangements. She did not know what arrangements meant. And she did not care. She just wanted her uncle back.

When they arrived at the clinic, Hannah overheard her mom whispering to Jones. "You're sure she'll be okay? Should I go with her?" She leaned in further to hear their conversation. "You're sure it's safe for her, Jones?" Taking a step back, Hannah's eyes shifted from side to side. *Why wouldn't it be safe?* She leaned back in and heard Jones assure her safety. Breathing a sigh of relief, she made a plan with her mom to stay with Jones and meet her mom back at the clinic at 3 p.m.

As she and Jones walked and talked along the dirt path to school, Hannah spotted a girl in the distance wearing a familiar purple dress. "Wilkister!" She called out. Running toward her with the bag of beads in her hands, Hannah called her name again. "Wilkister!"

Wilkister turned around. She carried a bucket of water on her head.

Hannah bent forward and put her hands on her knees while she caught her breath. She looked up. "I'm so sorry, Wilkister. I was so mean to you yesterday and I'm sorry."

Wilkister stared at her and said nothing.

Hannah stood up, still breathing heavily, and looked Wilkister in the eyes. "I really am sorry," she said. "Really."

"Is okay," Wilkister responded. This time it was her voice that was monotone. She said, "Jambo," to Jones and continued walking.

Hannah rushed up to her side. "Wilkister?" She touched Wilkister's shoulder. Wilkister stopped again. "I was mean to you because I miss my Uncle Brian. I had wanted to meet you with him." She looked down at the dirt path. "And I'm just sad."

Wilkister held the bucket in place with one hand and put her other arm around Hannah. "Is really okay, Hannah." Her voice was lighter, happier. "I miss him, too, and we be friends like he want. That make us all happy." She walked ahead, still hugging Hannah with one arm.

Not wanting to knock over the bucket, Hannah walked steady like a soldier. Jones removed it from Wilkister's head and put it on his. "You girls run ahead to school. I bring bucket."

"Asante!" Wilkister said. She grabbed Hannah's hand and they ran off toward school.

"What time does school start?" Hannah asked.

"It start when teacher and students arrive. Around 8 a.m. But I must fetch water. 10 kilometers walk. I prepare meal, then fetch water, then come to school."

"Whoa," Hannah said. "How long have you been up?"

Wilkister looked confused.

Hannah restated her question. "What time did you wake up this morning?"

"What you mean?" Wilkister asked. "Rooster crows at 5 a.m."

Hannah laughed out loud. The kind of laughter she had with Uncle Brian. "Oh," she said.

Bar Sauri Primary School—just ahead—had the same chipped, red dirt-covered white paint with blue trim that was on the bathroom stalls and the clinic. Hannah sensed a pattern. *Was that the only paint they had? Had it been donated?* There were no doors, just doorways, and no windows, just openings in the walls.

When they walked inside, all the kids came running up and circled around Hannah like she was a movie star—just like Sarah Oloo had treated her mom. They oohed and ahhed, giggled with each other and talked in a language Hannah did not understand. The dense crowd of children pushed into each other, closed in on Hannah, and grabbed at her forearms. She felt like Dorothy when she landed in

Oz. The Munchkins were all around her, and Uncle Brian was no longer there to be the scarecrow, the Tin Man or the lion to show her the way. And there was no yellow brick road. There were no roads at all.

"Children!" snapped the teacher. The kids scattered away. She fought her nervousness and smiled. Looking out the empty window, she saw Jones waving to her. She waved back. Knowing he was there, she felt more settled.

Wilkister introduced her to the teacher, Mr. Awuor. He wore a pressed white button-down shirt, a dark grey suit and purple tie. Seeming as though he had just picked his clothes up from a dry cleaner, he looked professional and distinguished. Hannah looked down at her shirt splattered with bugs and dirt and wondered how he remained so clean.

He invited Hannah to sit down next to Wilkister on a splintered wooden bench with an attached table. It would have sat about five kids across comfortably, but instead eleven jammed together. The room was hot and buggy, had no ventilation even though there were holes for doors and windows, and the kids were all trying to sit next to her, some little ones even climbing into her lap. They were drawn to her like magnets. One of the little girls sitting in her lap had a runny nose. She wiped her nose with her shirt and then snuggled into Hannah. Hannah noticed their gigantic smiles of perfectly straight white teeth.

She looked around at everyone and then at herself.

She was dressed in the most lightweight clothes she had brought—an off-white loose-fitting top and thin army-green pants. The kids wore uniforms; white shirts and blue shorts for the boys, white shirts and blue skirts for the girls. The shade of blue was the same bright peacock blue as the paint on the bathroom stalls, at the clinic, and at the school. None of them wore shoes except one boy who had on tattered sneakers two sizes too big. Hannah thought they all looked dirty, but she wondered if anyone felt quite as dirty as she did. The teachers were dressed differently, and it looked like they were prepared for a winter storm. One teacher wore a sweater with snowflakes and a big snowman on the front. Others had on heavy Patagonia jackets and seemed to be shivering. Hannah estimated it was probably about 85 degrees, but with the stench in the air and the sun beating down over them, it felt like over 100 degrees. She asked some of the kids about the weather and they told her it would get hot December, January and February. *It would get hot?* Outside the classroom, she could hear cows mooing, chickens clucking and stray dogs barking. A lizard was settled in the inside corner at the head of the classroom.

Hannah looked down at the girl with the runny nose, who was still in her lap, affectionately leaning into her and smiling at her. The children's kindness began to surpass Hannah's uneasiness and she smiled back.

The teacher announced that it was time for maths. He

said maths, not math, and Hannah giggled. She leaned to Wilkister, who had been sitting next to her, but was now about three people down since more kids had maneuvered themselves to be on the bench near Hannah, and said, "We call it math at home, just one math, not two or more maths!"

Wilkister laughed. "But is small for mathematics, yes? Small mathematics is maths!"

She was right. And why do we say short for rather than small for? Hannah giggled again.

Hannah noticed there was a chalkboard but did not see any chalk. The teacher had a frayed and worn textbook, pages yellowed with age, but there were no books for the kids. No paper. No pencils.

Mr. Awuor read aloud from the book while the children listened. He explained multiplication and addition. Hannah looked around. She thought about all of the stuff in her math classroom at home—pattern blocks, dice, place value charts, games. *These kids can't take notes or practice problems. How do they study for tests?*

A goat walked into the classroom and startled Hannah. Mr. Awuor looked at her and asked softly, "You do not have goats in America?"

Hannah looked around. All the kids wondered the same as their teacher. Not knowing what to say, she responded, "Well, um, not in our classroom, no." The goat walked out the doorway.

The children gathered into small groups and walked outside where there was a pile of sticks on the dirt ground. Each picking up a stick, the children went with their group of mixed ages and genders.

Mr. Awuor walked around and gave each group a problem aloud. As he walked from group to group, the students in each group worked out the problem together. Hannah stayed with Wilkister, who worked on double-digit multiplication. Keeping track of the numbers was difficult when they were scratched in the dry dirt with a jagged stick. And she noticed Wilkister making a few mistakes.

Taking a stick from the pile, Hannah stood off to the side of Wilkister's group and made graph paper in the dirt. The horizontal and vertical lines had created piles of dust so Hannah decided to spread them out. Having what seemed like all the dirt in the world to work with, she made the boxes bigger.

"Wilkister," she said. "Put the numbers in these boxes and it will help you keep them lined up." Hannah looked back at the problem Wilkister was working on and copied it over in the boxes on her dirt graph paper. Watching as Wilkister worked, Hannah made more dirt graph paper. Mr. Awuor took a stick and made some too. Eagerly waiting to do their problems on dirt graph paper, the children worked all afternoon.

Hannah thought about how well they would do

with real graph paper, pencils, calculators, math books and computers. Looking out into the dusty distance, she remembered Uncle Brian's words about progress and smiled.

Beach Balls and Frisbees

The following morning, Hannah filled her bag with the backpacks, beach balls, and Frisbees she and her mom had brought for the teachers and children. As they drove out to Sauri, she hoped her new friends would like what she brought.

Although Jones drove directly to the school that morning, Hannah decided to wait until lunchtime to give her gifts. That way, Wilkister and the other girls who were late because they had to fetch water would be there. She and her mom made a plan for her mom to go to the clinic until noon and then come to the school for lunch.

Lunch. Hannah thought back to the cafeteria at her school and vowed never again to complain about anything they served. At Bar Sauri Primary, some of the kids shared dusty green oranges. A few roasted ears of corn and then shared. Most had nothing. That day, Hannah had brought a banana. She had choked down chicken and kale the previous night and had eaten a piece of bread that morning. She was used to more food than that. And more choices. Peeling the banana and breaking it into thirds, she walked over to three small children and offered each of them a piece. Showing their beautiful white teeth, they smiled and giggled. "Asante sana! Asante sana! Asante sana!"

Remembering Uncle Brian teaching her the Swahili words for you're welcome, Hannah patted each on the head. "Karibu sana."

"You are nice girl, Hannah, to give your banana." Wilkister laughed out loud. "Hannah banana," she repeated. "Is funny! I call you Hannah Banana, is okay?"

"Sure," Hannah laughed. "Do you have a nickname?"

"Yes. Is Kister." She pronounced it Kees-tah.

"Oh, that's cute. Can I call you Kister?"

"Is okay, sure," she answered, smiling.

Hannah's mom walked up to the two girls and winked at Hannah. Introducing her mom to Wilkister, Hannah opened the beach balls. She had nowhere to put the packaging. She did not even have a pocket. *Where are the garbage cans? There's always trash burning in the distance.*

"Here." Her mom extended her hand. She took the plastic wrapping from Hannah and put it in the bag she was carrying. It felt like it was a thousand degrees outside.

The stink of burning trash and manure clogged the motionless air.

As Hannah blew up the beach ball, the kids gathered around in silence and it began to take shape. She took in another breath and felt dizzy, but resisted coughing and gasping in the smelly air. Her mom took the half-inflated ball and continued blowing it up. Taking a step back, Hannah watched the children. She had never before witnessed such pure joy as the children watched the purple, green, and white thick stripes become wider and wider. And she wondered who was happier in that moment—the kids or her. She looked up to the sky and thought of Uncle Brian. She smiled, knowing he was watching.

Hannah's mom finished blowing it up, put the stopper in, and handed the inflated ball back to Hannah with a smile. Hannah smiled back and looked around at the kids, who remained silent with anticipation. She tapped the ball up in the air and the children squealed with delight. They ran around and kept the ball in the air. Within minutes, they had covered the entire red dirt area that surrounded the school, and the ball never touched the ground. Hannah and her mom took turns blowing up the second beach ball in the pack. They tapped it in the air and the kids ran wild and free, happy.

"What if they pop?" Hannah whispered to her mom in a panic. "It's so hot here and there are sharp sticks lying around. What if they pop?" Her mother did not respond, only smiled and hugged her. Deciding to enjoy the moment, Hannah ran out and joined the kids.

She approached the Head Teacher, Mrs. Odhiambo, and asked if they had time for Frisbee. "Do you know Frisbee?"

Mrs. Odhimabo laughed and said, "Yes, yes is good. I know."

Hannah smiled and said, "Oh, good. Then we can have a little more time to play?"

"Play?" Mrs. Ohdiambo looked confused. She looked to Mr. Awour standing next to her. He shrugged his shoulders indicating his confusion. She looked back to Hannah. "You say, 'fresh beans,' yah? Is fresh beans or no?"

Hannah laughed. "No, it's called *Frisbee*," she enunciated. "It's a game. I'll show you." She pulled out a purple Frisbee from her backpack and tossed it across the way. No one caught it. They just watched it drop and still looked at it like it was the greatest invention they had ever seen. Running over to the fallen Frisbee, Hannah picked it up and lobbed it over to her mom who caught it. The kids cheered. The other kids who were still playing with the beach ball were still squealing. A little boy picked up the Frisbee and held it tight as if it was a precious gem. Looking up at Hannah, he took a breath determined to make it a solid toss. She caught it. His enormous smile brought tears to Hannah's eyes, but she refused to let herself cry. Instead, she tossed the Frisbee back to him and watched him throw it with his friends. She got the other two out of her backpack and tossed them out to the kids.

Lunchtime ran long that day. Before the kids were called back into class, the Head Teacher made an announcement. The beach balls and Frisbees were to be put away and only taken out for very special occasions. *Only for special occasions? They're just beach balls and Frisbees.* Feeling both happy and sad at the same time, Hannah went back to class.

After school that day, Hannah pulled collapsible backpacks she had gotten at her school store at home out of her bag and handed one each to the teachers and one to Mrs. Odhimabo. She watched as they put the backpacks on their heads. They stood up and walked around balancing the empty backpacks on their heads and complimenting each other. Unsure what to do, Hannah asked Mr. Awuor for his. He took it from his head and handed it to her. She showed everyone how to put their shoulders through the straps and said, "See? Hands-free."

The teachers oohed and ahhed, put the backpacks on their backs and said, "Is good hands-free!"

When she got outside, the kids called her over to show her some of their games. Her mom had not yet arrived back from the clinic, so when they asked Hannah to join, she happily went with them out to the dirt area surrounding the school.

"We play football and netball here," one student explained.

"Wait, I know you!" Hannah said. "What's your name?"

He looked around and stuttered. "Uh, Kiano."

"Kiano! That's right!"

"Yes," he agreed. "Is my name, Kiano."

She laughed. "No, I know you because my Uncle Brian showed me your picture. You have a wooden cell phone."

He smiled and pulled it out of his pocket. "Yes, allo?" He laughed. His expression softened and he said, "I sorry about your uncle, Hannah." She loved the way they all said Hannah the same, with the emphasis on NAH.

"Me, too." Changing the subject, she said, "I know football. We call it soccer back home. But what's netball?"

"We show you!"

There was a high pole with a metal hoop at the top that looked as though it might have had a basketball net at one point. Using only one hoop, the kids seemed to be playing basketball without dribbling. Realizing that's what netball was—basketball without dribbling—she wondered why there was only one hoop without a net. *Are there supposed to be two?* As she cheered for them, she noticed it was getting late. *Where's Mom? Where's Jones?*

"Want to play, Hannah?"

"Sure," she called out. As she ran to the makeshift dirt court, she looked over her shoulder toward the clinic.

They played a few games. "You are fast runner, Hannah," Kiano said to her as they walked off the court with the few other kids who were still there.

"Thank you," she said looking down at her feet. Usually not so shy, Hannah surprised herself by feeling giggly in Kiano's presence. He was a little taller than she and had a really cute smile. There was just something about Kiano. Being with him made Hannah feel happy.

They looked up and saw Jones's truck driving toward them. She could see Jones in the driver's seat, but not her mom. As Hannah ran toward the approaching truck, she waved bye to the kids. Wilkister and her brothers followed her.

"Where's my mom?" she asked Jones.

"She still at clinic. There is one man died and they wait for family there."

"Oh, I'm sorry." Hannah thought of Uncle Brian. "So, do you want me to go to the clinic and wait with you?"

"Is okay, Hannah. Your mum and Dr. Omundo are good. I wait with you. They are call me when is ready, is okay?"

"Yes," Hannah answered. It was getting dark. All the kids had gone home except for Wilkister, her brothers, and Kiano, who had walked up to join them.

Leaning her head into the driver's side of the truck, Hannah whispered, "Jones, can we drive them home?"

Wilkister overheard and giggled. "There is no road,

Hannah, nowhere for truck to drive. Is okay, we walk."

"See you tomorrow!" the four of them said and waved good-bye as they disappeared into the weathered stalks of maize.

Jones's phone rang about ten minutes after Hannah's friends had left. It was her mom telling them she was ready to be picked up at the clinic. They drove to get her.

"Thank you so much," she said to Dr. Omundo and climbed into the truck.

"Hannah, do you know a boy named Kiano?"

"Yeah," she said. "He and his friends just taught me how to play netball while we were waiting for you."

"I'm sorry you had to wait. It was a long day for you, too, huh?"

"No, that's all right. What about Kiano?"

"It was his uncle who died today. Remember the man who was at the clinic just about every day, coughing hard, with really glassy eyes?"

"Yes." Hannah responded. "I'm sorry."

"Me, too," she said. "They are such a nice family. Kiano's mom and grandmother came over to get his body. It took them a while because they stopped at a neighbor's house to borrow a bike."

"They took his body home *on a bike*?"

"Yes, and they said it wasn't too far. We offered to drive, but there is no way to get the truck through the maize fields. That's one of the things they . . ." She paused and corrected herself. "…we need to work out. There are obviously no ambulances. Bikes are the next best option."

Unsure what to say, Hannah responded simply, "Oh."

Prayer for Uncle Brian

It was the weekend. No school for two days. And Hannah still had not called her father. She wondered what the children did on the weekends. Having spent the previous three days with them, she figured they do a lot of chores—fetching water, harvesting crops. *I water the plants and do the dishes at home. I walk Livvy.* She guessed they also did some similar things—going to the market, hanging out with friends, sleeping late. She remembered Wilkister's rooster and laughed. *Well, maybe not sleeping late.*

Jones drove Hannah and her mom over to ICRAF. Hannah sat down next to Patrick and he told her about saying a prayer at the site of the bus accident. The fire had been devastating and there was nothing left but ashes. "It kind of was peaceful," he explained.

Hannah leaned in and hugged him. "Thank you for saying a prayer, Patrick." They sat in silence for a while.

"How about we all say prayer at Harvest Festival?" Patrick asked.

Hannah's mom perked up. "We could have a memorial service. Not taking away from the celebration of no one dying of hunger in a year, but adding to it with a prayer for Brian."

Sitting up but still nestled into Patrick, Hannah said, "Yes!"

When Patrick asked Hannah to tell him about school out in Sauri, she asked him a few questions she had about Bar Sauri Primary School. "What about school supplies like paper, pencils and books? There were some books, but not a lot. And most of them were for really little kids."

"Donations to schools and some government aid, but never enough from government. Is right, Hannah, never enough."

She thought again about the $50 for a visa and shrugged.

Patrick explained that secondary education was like high school, but it cost an annual fee of 16,800 KES per student. Hannah figured that was about $200. "What?" she asked. "Are you kidding me? How can anyone pay that?"

"Actually, Hannah, many people send children, most of boys, to secondary school. They work harvest, save money for education. Is important."

"Oh," she said. *Girls hardly get to go to school. Some boys get to go. And then what?* "Does anyone get to go to college?"

"Not many. No, not many."

"So." She tried to understand. "Kids work hard in school, their families spend their money to get them to secondary school where they also work hard and then have spent all their money and they end up back in Sauri without a job anyway?"

"Yes," he answered.

Hannah nodded. She thought about her parents, who met in college and ended up back in the town where her dad had grown up. *They chose to move there. But they had options.* She asked her mom for her phone. "I'm going to call Dad, okay?" Taking in a deep breath, she took the phone from her mom and walked out the door to the front porch. She got his voicemail and wondered if he did not want to talk to her either. "Hi Dad. Just calling you... Um... Bye." She hung up the phone.

Back at the Classic that night, the phone rang. Hannah picked up. "Hi Dad."

"Hey, Sweetie."

Silence. *Please don't ask about the weather.*

"Mom says you've been spending time in Sauri."

"We have." She smiled. "Mom's been helping out at the clinic and I've been going to school. The kids are awesome, Dad. And the teachers."

"That's great."

Silence.

"It must be really hot there, huh?" *Ugh.*

"Can you come for Harvest Festival, Dad? Please? We're going to say a prayer for Uncle Brian."

"Oh, that's really nice!" Hannah held her breath hoping he would change his mind. "But who would take care of Livvy?"

She shrugged. And she could not stand it when he dodged her questions. "The neighbors can take her. And you know it. They've taken her plenty of times before."

"I need to be here for work. And I need to take care of Livvy. But you can tell me about it when you get home, okay? Okay, Hannah?"

"Yes, Dad. Okay."

"How are you doing other than that? Is everything okay? Is Mom feeling better?"

"If you really wanted to know, you'd just come here and see for yourself." She put the phone down. "Mom!" she called. "Dad wants to talk to you."

Later that night, Hannah, her mom and Beary were lying across the bed talking. Hannah moved her hand along the side of the mattress and noticed Grace had washed the sheets. "These sheets are so clean!" She leaned over and sniffed. "And they smell so good!" Grace washed everything by hand.

"I wish we were clean and smelled good," her mom said. They both laughed.

"Things are getting better, Mom."

Her mom turned her body toward Hannah and Beary, and nestled into her pillow. "I'm so glad, Hannah. Thank you for staying. I really needed to stay and am sorry if I forced you. I know this has been so hard on you."

"It's been hard on all of us. Everyone loved Uncle Brian so much. And in a weird way, that's what is making me so happy. We came here to help them. Or at least that's why I thought we came here. But they're helping us just as much. If not more."

"They really know a lot about taking care of each other here, don't they?"

"They sure do."

Clinic with Kiano

"You're going to walk with Kiano to the clinic after school today, Hannah, all right?" her mom asked Monday morning on the drive to Sauri.

"Why? I mean, I don't mind at all, I'm just wondering."

"Dr. Omundo went to Nairobi last night for more medicine, and we're really busy with all the people coming in. After her brother died last week, Kiano's mom started helping at the clinic. She is very smart and knows a lot about medicine. She told us she went to secondary school and loved science. She said she could come again today, so we thought you and Kiano could help organize the medicine that Dr. Omundo brings back. Does that sound good?"

"Yes!"

A game of soccer was already underway when Jones dropped Hannah at school. She jumped in. The only one wearing shoes, she was careful when going for the ball. She kicked the top part of the ball to avoid hitting her opponent's bare foot, and she tripped and went skidding across the harsh, dusty ground. The kids stopped the game and ran toward her. "You are okay, Hannah?"

"Yes," she said, and got up. "I'm fine." She looked to her opponent, who she had kicked as she fell. "I'm sorry, Eunice. I was trying not to kick you and I ended up kicking you anyway. And falling on my face!"

Eunice patted Hannah's arm and said, "Is okay, Hannah."

The bell rang and they walked to the school building. Hannah realized the bases of both of her palms were raw, oozing minuscule spurts of blood. They stung as she wiped them against her army green pants. She wanted so badly to wash them under cold water and put on Neosporin with a Band-Aid. She knew there was some in the clinic but felt like a baby going all the way there for such minor cuts. There was no sink in the classroom, no water fountain to run her hands under, no school nurse to visit, nothing. So she walked into the room, took her seat on the splintery bench and desk, and tried not to touch anything.

"I'm sorry about your uncle, Kiano," she whispered when he walked in.

"Is okay, thank you." His voice was quiet.

"We both have uncles who died, so if you want to talk about it." She stopped talking and looked down. "I mean, it's just really sad and I'm really sorry." She felt her cheeks burn and started to cry.

He put his hand on her shoulder. She looked up at him and he was smiling. "Wilkister say you are so good, but you know, I think she is very right." He looked toward the ground and said, "And I am happy you here." Her cheeks blushed.

Hannah looked around and noticed the faces of the children around her. Some were familiar from last week. Others were new. Some she had seen a few times only. There were always more boys than girls. Kids would come to school when they could—so they would study and learn together at various ages. She leaned over to Kiano who had sat two people down from her on the bench. "Where's Wilkister?" she whispered.

"Wilkister? Ah, Wilkister have malaria. Maybe, is malaria is bad for her now."

"What? Wilkister has malaria?" Hannah asked, frightened. The teacher gave her a look. She stopped talking.

"Is okay, Hannah. Is medicine for her. To get her better," Kiano assured her after the teacher had started working with a group of students on the other side of the room.

"Where?" she whispered.

"At clinic, yah. Is okay. We make sure with my mum."

Hannah thought of her malaria pills back at the Classic. She was to take one pill once a week and would not have to worry about contracting malaria. And just to be extra cautious, she had a bed net to keep the mosquitoes away. *The bed net for Wilkister! It's still in the back of the truck. Does she even need it now? Can you get malaria again? Do you ever get rid of it?*

"Is okay, Hannah, we make sure," Kiano reassured her.

Hannah had brought fruit from a trip to the market over the weekend and shared it with some of the kids at lunch. There were two little boys sitting by themselves under a tree. She sat down next to them and peeled a banana. She broke it into thirds, a piece for each of them and one for herself. She handed each of the boys a piece and they responded with a giggly "Asante sana, Hannah!"

She smiled back and said, "Karibu sana." As she opened her mouth to take a bite of her piece, an elderly lady appeared out of nowhere. She had gray scraggly hair, was missing a few front teeth, and wore a blue shirt caked with dust and a torn red patterned wrap skirt that fell to her bare ankles and feet. Rubbing her stomach, she stared with sad eyes at what was left of the banana. It was the last of the fruit Hannah had brought for lunch and she had not eaten anything yet. And she was hungry. She thought of the eating schedule back at home—breakfast before school, lunch provided at school, and two snack times built into the school day. Kids at her school would bring snacks from home. She smiled and handed the banana to the woman, who smiled widely, further wrinkling her worn black skin and showing her remaining teeth, which were brown along the edges and yellow up toward the gums. "Asante," she whispered fragilely and scurried off, already showing energy from the nutrients her unexpected piece of banana would soon provide.

After school that day, Kiano approached Hannah. "You are ready to go to clinic?" he asked.

She smiled and nodded. This was the first time she had walked anywhere without her mom, Jones, Grace, Patrick, or Uncle Brian. She felt a little nervous, but she trusted Kiano and was happy to spend time with him.

As they walked further away from the school toward the clinic, there were more bushes and trees scattered around, creating red dirt paths leading in different directions. Hannah's sense of direction had always been nonexistent, even at home where there were street signs and landmarks. The paths wound and intertwined with patches of maize. Everything looked the same. As she pushed aside the withering leaves of the stalks of maize to follow Kiano, she smelled fresh produce, like a farmer's market. She inhaled deeply through her nose, taking in every bit of the first good scent in Sauri.

A little boy, about five years old, dressed in weathered

dirty blue shorts and a white shirt—the Bar Sauri Primary School boys' uniform—was crying hard when they passed him along a dirt path. Hannah watched as Kiano spoke with the boy in Luo, their tribal language.

"What happened?" she asked Kiano. "Why is he crying?"

"He lose his money for to buy book at school. He cannot find anywhere in maize field. His grandmother give him special 10 shilling and he lose."

Kiano tsk-tsked his irresponsibility. Hannah was surprised at Kiano's reaction. *He's only a little kid. And that's about 12 cents.* Hannah reached in her pants pocket to see if she had any change. She did. *Should I offer him the money? I didn't even know I had it.* "Kiano?" she whispered, "I have 10 shillings and can give him the money, but is that okay?"

Kiano smiled and nodded. "Yes, Hannah, is good."

Hannah reached out her palm to show the boy the coin and said, "This is for you, for your book." She smiled.

His sweet little teary face shined as bright as the hot African sun. He smiled and took the coin from her. "Asante sana!" he called out as he ran through the maize fields and back to school, clutching the coin in his little fist.

They walked together past the crowd of sick patients through the doorway of the clinic.

"Hey, Han!" her mom said.

"Mom, this is Kiano, my friend from school."

"Oh, hello, Kiano. It's so nice to meet you."

He smiled, shook her hand, and said, "Allo, Mrs. Higgins. Is nice meet you." He walked over to the other woman in the room who was treating a patient and said, "And, Hannah, this my mum."

After his mom finished with the patient, Hannah extended her right hand. "Hello, Mrs. Oluoch. Jambo."

"Allo, sweet Hannah," she said. "Is nice to see you. I hear from your mum and Kiano." She patted Kiano on the head and said, "I hear good thing. So many good thing." Hannah looked at Kiano with a huge smile on her face. He was looking down at the ground.

"What medicine do you want us to put away? How do you want us to organize it?" Hannah asked, looking around for boxes. "And where's Dr. Omundo?"

Her mom walked to the next patient in line. She talked as she examined him. "The medicine that was supposed to be there wasn't. Dr. Omundo spent today on a wild goose chase and didn't find the shipment."

Kiano leaned into Hannah. "Is what a wild goose chase? Where is wild gooses?"

Hannah laughed out loud and said, "I'll tell you later." She looked back to her mom, who was equally amused.

"A wild goose chase," her mom explained, "just means he looked everywhere and couldn't find the medicine." She laughed again and continued talking. "Patrick has a friend in Nairobi, so Dr. Omundo is going to stay there tonight and hope it turns up tomorrow."

"Where do you think it went? Was it supposed to be at a pharmacy, or was it a shipment to the post office?"

"It was put aside for us at a pharmacy. The people there promised to have it for us tomorrow, so we'll keep our fingers crossed." She looked at Kiano and crossed her fingers. "Means good luck," she said to him with a smile.

He crossed his fingers as she had and repeated, "Is good luck," with a big smile.

Hannah's mom moved through the line of patients while Hannah and Kiano sorted through the few remaining boxes. His nose was pressed up to the boxes as he read the labels. "Kiano?" Hannah asked. "Do you need glasses?"

"Glasses?"

She took the right side of her frames in her fingers and moved it up and down. "Glasses. Like these. To see better."

"Oh. I do not know."

"Well, can you see?"

He shrugged his shoulders. "I do not know."

Thinking about all the people she had met, the only one Hannah had seen with glasses had been Dr. Omundo. *They don't have glasses out here.*

She took hers off and handed them to him. "Here, try these on."

He put them on and jerked his head back. Blinking his eyes several times, he took them off and handed them back. He shook his head. "Whoa." They both laughed.

As the last person walked out, Hannah looked at her mom and said, "Will they all be okay until tomorrow? And, Mom, did you know Wilkister has malaria?"

"Yes," she answered. "I was going to tell you that on the way home, but don't worry. Her grandmother was at the clinic early and got medicine for her. She should be back at school in a few days."

"Oh, good," Hannah responded. "I'm just glad her grandmother was here early." She paused and thought for a moment. She looked up at her mom. "What if she hadn't been?"

"She was," her mom answered, smiling.

"But what if she hadn't been?"

"But she was, Hannah. She was."

Kiano and his mom were getting ready to leave. "Bye-bye, Hannah," his mom said, and put her arm around Hannah's shoulders.

"Bye," Hannah said with a smile. "Thank you."

"Is thank me? For why?" she asked.

"Thank you for helping my mom," she said. "And all of the people who need you."

"Ah, is okay. We need each other, is right?"

"Yes," Hannah agreed. "Yes, we do."

Two Showers and Extra Medicine

Uncharacteristically quiet during the ride home, Hannah could not believe the clinic was already out of medicine. She and her mom had brought almost an entire duffel bag less than two weeks earlier. And she knew if she got really sick, they would leave. They would be leaving in just over a week anyway, but they could get an earlier flight. In Sauri, people waited in line at a clinic where they were out of medicine. *It's so unfair.* She hoped Dr. Omundo would be able to locate the medicine and get it back to Sauri the next day.

"Why you are quiet, Hannah?" Jones asked her.

"No reason," she answered.

"Really is no reason?"

"I was just wishing there was enough medicine for

everyone," she said. "And eyeglasses for people who can't see." She nudged her mom who was resting. "Kiano couldn't see anything on those boxes!"

"Oh, is good wish," Jones said. "Is my wish, too." Hannah looked up at him and smiled. "My another wish to see my family is true."

"What?" Hannah perked up.

Meredith sat up and leaned over to listen. "You're going to see Rebecca and Anthony?"

"Yes," he said with his typical huge smile. "But no worry, Patrick drive you to Sauri while I be gone to Kitui."

Hannah and her mom both insisted they were not at all concerned about that. They wanted to hear more about his trip. "When's the last time you saw Rebecca and Anthony?" Hannah asked.

"Is six weeks before I went home," he answered. "Long time with not my family. And next I come back to my family here, is you!"

They pulled into the Classic and Hannah leaned over and hugged him. "I'll miss you, Jones," she said.

"I do not leave until a few days," he said and parked the truck. "And I come back in some days soon."

Grace was inside preparing kale and potatoes for dinner. She heard Hannah and her mom walk in and looked directly at Hannah with a twinkle in her eye. "Water?" Hannah asked.

"Yes, is water today!" she answered.

"Asante sana!" Hannah cheered and ran upstairs.

At dinner, Hannah could not stop thinking about Wilkister. "Are you sure Wilkister's grandmother took enough medicine?"

"She took enough to get her better, yes," her mom answered.

"But, I mean, shouldn't she take enough so she has it for the next time Wilkister gets sick?"

"Well, no, because there would have been even less there for the others who needed it today, Hannah."

"Oh," Hannah looked down.

Grace chimed in and said, "Is only what you need you take."

Hannah remembered tipping at the Mon Ami Club and the community food program and how it had been a year since anyone in Sauri had died of hunger. And at the clinic, they were to take only what medicine they needed and there was still not enough. *Leave what you can. Take only what you need.* Hannah sighed. Never having thought of herself as a selfish person, she questioned whether she could follow this rule for everything.

As they got ready for bed, Hannah said to her mom, "I should have waited to take a shower. I'm all hot and dusty again."

"You could take another quick one."

"Nah."

"What's the matter, Han?"

She climbed in under the bed net and reached for Beary. She put him next to her as she laid her head on the pillow. "I just feel bad." She started to cry.

Her mom put down the medical papers she was reading and put her head down on the pillow facing Hannah. "About what?"

"I want two showers. I want extra medicine for Wilkister." She was sobbing. "And I don't want to take two showers here but I would at home without even thinking about it. And what if Wilkister's grandmother hadn't come in the morning? I know she did, but what if she hadn't?"

"She *did* get there soon enough." Her mom brushed her hand through Hannah's clean hair and softened her response. "She did get there, but you're right, it's scary to think if she hadn't, isn't it?"

Hannah nodded and stared through the inside of the bed net to the chipped paint on the wall. Her breath steadied and she blinked a few final tears before she fell asleep.

Necklaces, Hair Ties, and Beetles

Wilkister was back at school when Hannah arrived the following morning. "I have present for you, Hannah Banana!" She handed Hannah a necklace.

It was beautiful. The beads—blue, purple, green and white—were intricately woven into strands and clasped with a tiny gold twist cylinder in the back. Hannah hugged her new friend. "Thank you, Kister! I love it!"

As she carefully clasped it around her neck, she realized her hair tie had fallen out. She moved her hair so it fell in front of her right shoulder and then leaned to get it completely out of the way so she could fasten the clasp securely. She put her head upright again and felt the smooth beads with both hands. "I love it, Wilkister!" she exclaimed.

"Karibu sana, Hannah."

"Uncle Brian told me you made bracelets. I didn't know you made necklaces, too."

Wilkister nodded and smiled.

"And how are you feeling? I am so sorry you were sick."

"Is okay. The medicine from the clinic is good."

Mrs. Odihambo rang the bell and the children walked inside and sat down. *How does Wilkister make up the work she missed? There are no notes to copy, no homework to email, no computers to send or receive an email, no phones.* As Hannah's mind wandered off, an enormous bug—bigger than any bug she had ever seen—flew into the classroom. It sounded like an old lawn mower. Hannah screamed. She looked around, eyes wide, mouth open, shocked. No one else flinched. "What is that?" she asked, cringing.

"A beetle," a few kids said softly.

"That is *not* a beetle!" she said laughing, but still squirming because it had crawled closer in her direction. "Do they sting?" she stuttered as it crawled closer and closer.

"Yes," Kiano said protectively. He stood up and shooed it out the open door.

After school ended, the kids walked outside and Hannah asked Wilkister, "How long have you had malaria?"

"I have malaria three years now and is okay." She changed the subject. "You were scared of beetle today, yah?"

"That was not a beetle!" Hannah insisted again, laughing. "That thing was enormous and it sounded like a machine!"

Wilkister laughed and asked, "Do you keep animal at home, Hannah?"

"Yes, we have a dog. She's a Tibetan Terrier named Livvy. I miss her."

"What is Tibetan Terrier?"

"She's really furry. She even has big eyebrows, a mustache and a beard!"

Wilkister laughed. "That is funny. And you miss it? I would not miss my chickens. Or my rooster!"

"I can't wait to tell her all about you and the kids here," Hannah said.

"Tell who? Livvy? It is not a dog?"

Hannah laughed and felt her cheeks turn red. "Yes, she is a dog. And yes, I do talk to her," she admitted.

"A dog who understand English? That is very funny. When I come to America, I will teach him Swahili."

"Livvy is a she, Wilkister, she's a girl!" Hannah said, giggling at the thought of Livvy being bilingual. She gently touched the beads of her new necklace. "I feel so lucky to have such a special present from you, Wilkister."

Wilkister smiled.

"My best friend at home is named Emily. She makes really pretty earrings. I wish you two could meet. You would really like each other."

"Is easy to make necklace. And bracelet. I could teach you and you teach Emily."

"Really?" Hannah asked. "You think I could learn how to make them?" She touched her necklace again. "You think I could make ones this good?" Kiano walked up to them and the girls continued talking.

"Sure. You come home with me after school tomorrow and I show you?"

"Um," Hannah felt a twinge of nerves in her stomach. "I would love to, Wilkister. Is it okay if I ask my mom first?"

"Sure, is okay."

"But how can I let you know if I can stay after school or not?"

"You just come. And if you not here, you can't come."

Hannah laughed. "That makes things easy. Thanks!" *They're so easy-going here.* "I'll tell you at school tomorrow, okay?" Wilkister nodded. Jones drove up to take Hannah and Kiano to the clinic.

"See you tomorrow, Wilkister!" Hannah and Kiano called out as they climbed into the truck. Kiano did not take his eyes off of Jones. "I want learn to drive like you, Jones."

Jones laughed. "Yes, I teach you."

"Is true, you teach me?"

"Sure, is true. I teach you."

"Asante, Jones," he said and grinned at Hannah.

She smiled back and looked out to the horizon and thought of Uncle Brian. *We help each other here.*

After dinner that evening, Hannah asked to call her dad. "Sure!" Her mom responded.

Hannah walked away from the picnic table area and called home.

"Hello?"

"Hi Dad!"

"Hannah! Hi!"

"The last time we talked, I didn't really get to tell you about school. And the clinic." She told him about Wilkister and Kiano, and making graph paper in the dirt. She told him about running out of medicine and Kiano needing glasses. She told him about laughter over the wild goose chase and the beetle in the classroom. "And Livvy is going to be bilingual!"

He laughed like she had not heard in a long time.

"Wilkister is going to teach her Swahili."

He laughed harder.

"I'm glad you're making friends, Hannah. I knew you would. Everyone loves you. You're just like Brian."

"Everyone loves you, too, Dad," she said.

She could hear him sigh but could tell he was smiling.

"I should have gone," he said. "I would have gotten to

145

spend time with my brother. And I would have been there with you and Mom."

Tears filled in Hannah's eyes. "It's not too late, Dad. You can still come."

"It is too late. But I can't wait to have you guys home next week. You'll be able to tell me all about it. And you're taking pictures, right?"

"Yes, I'm taking lots of pictures," she said. "I even got pictures of the beetle."

He laughed again. It was good to hear him laughing.

"Good. Can't wait to see them. And you. I love you, Hannah."

"Love you, too, Dad."

Friends

Hannah and Wilkister walked through the maize fields to Wilkister's hut after school the next day. Hannah's mom had said she could go as long as Hannah and Wilkister stayed together until she and Jones picked her up.

The stalks were so high and dense, Hannah could not see over or through them. Dull green husks bordered with dust, Hannah could smell the freshness of corn on the cob. With no road signs or roads, Wilkister weaved through the maize quickly as if it were a game.

Hannah thought of what a cool app or video game this would be. It would be called Maize Maze and kids would have to get from one place to another without getting lost. They would learn about the awesomeness of small African towns like Sauri. The location destinations would be school, the clinic, the flour mill, Wilkister's hut, and the guy who sometimes sells bread along the main dirt path. He would be worth a lot of points because he would only show up on the screen from time to time. They would score bonus points for helping with harvests and getting medicine to the clinic. Delighted with her plan, Hannah decided she would get in touch with Apple as soon as she got home.

"Hey Wilkister. Have you ever heard of video games?"

"Video game? No," she answered.

Hannah explained about apps and video games. She would give creative credit to both of them. Maize Maze, created by Wilkister Omolo and Hannah Higgins.

As she walked through the wood slatted door into Wilkister's circular shaped hut, Hannah worked every muscle in her face not to react. The hut was made of mud and sticks. Maybe even some cow dung. Its tin, wood, and straw roof was held together with sod. Hannah wondered if it leaked when it rained. She smelled manure. She thought of the poop-scented stickers her science teacher had put on their homework and remembered how class had been dismissed because the smell was so bad. This was much worse. Mosquitoes flew around. There was a kitchen to her left when she walked in—a counter with a bucket of water and a tin bowl. In the corner on the ground was a small area for cooking over charcoal.

"We make chapati, Hannah. Is dinner."

"Oh, good!" she said. "What's chapati?"

With the sun already setting, it was difficult to see inside. Wilkister took Hannah by the hand. "Come, Hannah. I show you my room."

Wilkister shared a bed with her baby sister and her two brothers shared a bed on the opposite side of the room. There was a window with no glass in between their beds. Outside were the chickens and rooster.

Wilkister's dani—her grandmother—slept on a couch in the main room. The two couches were hard and thin, like old futons, and padded with scratchy wool blankets. Hannah wondered when they would ever need wool blankets. Then she thought back to the sweaters and jackets the teachers wore in 85-degree weather.

"Dani, this Hannah."

Hannah and Wilkister's grandmother exchanged greetings.

"You are watch Evelyn, is good?"

"Yes, yes," Dani said and took Wilkister's baby sister with her outside.

"Where are your brothers?" Hannah asked.

"They work harvest. They come back for dinner."

"Oh," Hannah said.

"You want make necklace and bracelet then make chapati, is good? And ugali?"

"Sure! What's ugali?"

Wilkister giggled. "I show you later."

From a small wooden cabinet in her room, Wilkister got out a tin bucket of beads and the bag of beads Hannah had given her. She took out string and two clasps. "I put together clasp for you," she said as she tied the clasp to the strings and pulled it tight. "Now I clasp for me." She did the same thing over again. "Then we start bead like this." She chose several beads and weaved them through the strings intricately, creating a beautiful pattern.

"Whoa," Hannah said. "Hang on. How did you do that?"

"I show you again." Wilkister took more beads out of the bucket and wove them through the strings, repeating the pattern perfectly.

"Ugh," Hannah sighed. "I know how to put beads on a string, but not like this. And these beads are so pretty, but so small." She watched Wilkister over and over again, and then tried it herself. She messed up, loosened the beads from the string and tried again. She squinted in the dim light. Wilkister got up and returned with the gas lamp. Looking at the necklace under the light, Hannah noticed her beads were a little mismatched.

"How long does it take you to finish one?"

Wilkister thought for a moment. "About half a day, but sometime less time."

"Wow," Hannah said. She reached up to her neck and touched the beads on the necklace Wilkister had made for her. "I have something to tell you, Kister. Can you keep a secret?"

"A secret not to tell somebody? Okay," she answered.

"I am serious," Hannah said, smiling.

"Is okay. What is secret?" Wilkister asked.

"I have a crush on Kiano," Hannah said shyly. "But seriously, Wilkister, don't tell anyone."

She looked at Hannah, puzzled. "Why you want crush Kiano? That hurt him, yah?"

Hannah laughed. "No, I am not going to crush him. I *have* a crush on him. That means I like him."

"Oh," Wilkister said laughing. "Oh, I understand. You like Kiano. Ha, ha, is funny."

"What's so funny about it?" Hannah asked.

"I no know. He is nice boy, is good to crush."

"*Have* a crush," Hannah corrected.

"Have a crush," Wilkister repeated. "On Kiano."

There was a knock at the door. Wilkister got up and answered it. Hannah heard Kiano's voice and her heart skipped a beat. *Did he hear us talking? There's no glass in the window.*

She walked out of the room pretending she had not said a word. "Hi, Kiano!"

"Allo, Hannah!" he said. "I finish work harvest for today. What you guys are doing?"

"Making necklaces," Hannah answered. Wilkister giggled and Hannah tried to ignore her. "And bracelets."

Kiano looked at Hannah. She said, "Do you want to hang out with us?" Unable to imagine a boy wanting to hang out and make jewelry, she hoped he would.

"Sure," he said and they walked back into Wilkister's room.

"What you do is fun back home, Hannah?" Kiano asked. "Since we know is not to make necklace." Hannah looked at her mismatched beads and jabbed Kiano in the arm.

"Very funny!" she said as she untangled more beads from her string. "I really like to run. I am on the cross-country team at school. That means we…"

"I know cross-country!" Kiano interrupted. "I watch Olympic Games and Kenya runners are fast."

"They sure are!" Hannah agreed. "I love watching the Olympics. And yes, Kenyan runners always get the gold medals." She thought for a moment. No electricity. No TV. No Internet. No computer. "Where do you watch?" she asked.

"My uncles take me sometime to Kisumu where there is Mon Ami Club."

Hannah dropped her necklace and beads scattered everywhere. Crawling around on the dirt floor collecting the beads, she said, "I've been to Mon Ami Club! And my Uncle Brian used to go there all the time."

"My uncle use to go there," Kiano said sadly. "But I still go with my other uncle the next time Olympic Games."

"That's really fun," she said. "I wish I could come back here for the next Olympic Games." She thought for a moment and said, "Have you heard of a marathon? There's the New York City Marathon every November and I go sometimes, but even if I don't go, I always watch it on TV. I think the winners are usually from Kenya."

"Yes, is marathon in New York City," both Wilkister and Kiano confirmed. "And we hear when is winner to Kenya."

Hannah had collected all of the spilled beads. She put them back in the tin bucket and looked at her necklace of loose string, lumpy beads, and no pattern. Wilkister's was beautiful.

Wilkister looked over to Hannah and then continued working. "I finish this for you take to Emily and I keep yours for me."

"No," Hannah said, even though she secretly wanted Wilkister's pretty one. "I can finish this one on the plane home next week. And I promised Grace I would make her a bracelet."

"No, no," Wilkister insisted. "I want yours. It is good memory to you. I can make necklace for Emily and you make bracelet for Grace. She will want from you."

Hannah laughed. "Well," she said, "I know Emily will want yours instead of mine." They all laughed. "And yes, I want to make the bracelet for Grace. You'll show me how?" Wilkister nodded.

"We make bracelet for Grace and I finish later necklace for Emily." Wilkister attached string to the clasp and handed the beads to Hannah one by one. "Thanks, Kister."

After handing Hannah the final beads, Wilkister adjusted the clasp and handed the finished bracelet to Hannah. She stood up and wiped her hands against her skirt. Hannah's eyes sparkled as she held the bracelet carefully in her hands.

"We go make chapati now, is okay?"

Hannah and Kiano followed Wilkister to the kitchen area. Wilkister's dani had left the ingredients in the tin bowl on the counter so all Wilkister had to do was mix them together. "What is chapati, Kister?"

"I show you. You put this and mix and you have duff."

"What's duff?" Hannah asked.

"You know, is duff," she said.

"Duff," Kiano repeated to Hannah.

Hannah's heart raced a little. *Should I know what duff is?*

Wilkister and Kiano exchanged looks. Wilkister said, "Hannah, you know duff." She spelled it out, "D-o-u-g-h. Is duff."

Hannah burst out laughing. "Oh, dough! It's pronounced *dough*."

"Ah, dough," Wilkister and Kiano both repeated and they all laughed.

Handing Hannah another bowl, Wilkister asked her to mix it. Hannah looked in the bowl and tried not to gag. "What is this?"

"Is ugali. Flour and water. You mix."

As Hannah stirred, she asked, "Do you cook it?"

Wilkister rolled out the dough from her mixture into circles and lit the charcoal with a match. Sitting on a tiny stool and cooking the chapati like pancakes, she laughed. "No, is ugali. Just eat like that. Sometimes with cow's meat." Hannah tried not to make a face. "Hannah Banana, tell Kiano about your dog who I teach Swahili." She giggled.

Hannah said, "Oh yeah, I have a dog. A Tibetan Terrier named Livvy. She's awesome."

"And she learn to speak Swahili?" he asked.

Hannah looked over at Wilkister and then answered Kiano's question. "Yes. She only speaks English, so Wilkister is going to teach her Swahili." Wilkister's laughter echoed from the tiny area where she was frying the chapati.

"I have dog, too," Kiano said. "His name is Jimmy."

"Really?" Hannah asked. "Can I meet him?"

"Sure, is good. We go meet Jimmy. Is okay Kister?"

"Yah, is good, is good," Wilkister answered.

The most delicious food Hannah had tasted since she got to Kenya, chapati was like warm pita bread, scrumptious. She left the bowl of ugali on the counter.

They each had a piece of chapati. Then Wilkister put the rest in a plastic container for dinner. They walked out the wooden door and through the maize fields several minutes, winding their way around. Hannah wondered how people ever found their way anywhere out there.

As they approached his hut, Kiano called out, "Jimmy!" and a medium sized light brown smiling mutt ran toward him. He reminded Hannah of the dog, Sandy, from the play, *Annie*. She squatted down and he put his front paws on her knees, licked her face and shook all over with excitement. Looking up she said, "No way! This is his house?" Kiano laughed and nodded.

Jimmy lived in a doghouse behind their hut made from pieces of plywood and slats of tin for a roof, just like the old flour mill. The tin roof extended on one side like an awning that reached over the open side of the doghouse for Jimmy to be able to lounge and watch over Kiano and his family. Jimmy and his cool doghouse made Hannah like Kiano even more.

Hannah heard what sounded like pebbles hitting the tin roof of Jimmy's doghouse. She felt drops of water on her head and arms and looked up. The sky had turned a deep, stormy grey. The rain caught all three of them completely off guard. It fell steady—there was no wind blowing it from side to side—but still, a complete downpour within seconds.

Jimmy escaped into his doghouse.

Kiano said, "Come inside."

They ran into his hut. "That rain came from nowhere!" Hannah exclaimed. "It's been sunny since I got here."

"Do you think rain is much?" Wilkister asked.

"Uh, yeah," Hannah insisted.

"You come back visit to April and May. That is rainy season. This just little, light sprinkle," she giggled.

Rainwater poured inside the glassless window near the kitchen. Wilkister started to cough. "Are you feeling all right?" Kiano asked.

"Yah, is good."

Hannah did not believe her. She wished she could go to their medicine cabinet and get something to help Wilkister's cough. *Medicine cabinet. There was no bathroom for a medicine cabinet anyway.*

Kiano's hut looked exactly the same as Wilkister's except for an old fashioned radio sitting on the table. "What a cool radio!" Hannah said.

Kiano smiled. "Is my new radio. I hear news and songs on it."

New radio? It looks ancient.

"How does it work without electricity?"

He cranked a lever on its side and they heard faint static. He continued turning and Hannah heard music. "Wait!" She listened closely. Putting her ear up to the radio, the music got louder. "I know this song! Swing Swing!"

Kiano and Wilkister gasped. "How you know Swing Swing? Is good song, yah?"

Hannah thought of Uncle Brian singing random words. "The best," she said.

A Good Idea?

The rain had stopped. Kiano walked Wilkister and Hannah back to Wilkister's hut and wished them a good night. Wilkister and Hannah went back to her room to work on the necklaces before Hannah's mom arrived. Evelyn and Wilkister's dani were playing inside.

"I want do something for Brian," Wilkister blurted out.

"What do you mean?"

"I think about Brian is all the time."

"Me, too," Hannah sighed. "But what do you mean you want to do something for him. Like what?"

"We need celebrate him. We need remember him."

"Yes!" Hannah said. "But how?"

She thought for a moment. "We can take bus to where he die. We can give flowers where he die."

"That's a nice idea." Hannah's voice trailed off. She thought about Patrick going to the site of the bus accident and saying a prayer.

"Or we make road better."

Hannah stood up. Her beads went all over the place. "That's it! We could make the road better!" She picked up the beads. Wilkister helped her.

"How we do that?

"We need to talk to Sarah Oloo."

"Sarah Oloo? That is who?"

"The Chief Architect of the Ministry of Roads and Public Works for all of Kenya!"

"How we talk to her?"

"We need to go to Nairobi." She bit her lower lip. "Take a bus to Nairobi."

Wilkister's eyes widened. "I come too?"

"Sure, as long as your grandmother says you can."

Pacing around the room, Hannah wished she had her phone—or a pen and paper—to write down her thoughts. Instead she made her list out loud hoping she would remember. "We need to call her." *How do we find her phone number without Internet? Maybe Patrick can help us.* "We need to get bus tickets to Nairobi." *That will be the same route Uncle Brian took.* Her lips quivered and her eyebrows arched. She continued talking. "We should buy Sour Patch Kids." *I haven't seen any candy since we got here. Maybe in*

Nairobi they'll have more stores? Can we go by ourselves, just Mom, Wilkister, and me? Will Mom let us?

"Is what sour kids?" Wilkister asked.

"Allo? Wilkister? Hannah?" They heard Jones knocking at the door. Wilkister opened it. Soggy on the outside and leaking through the inside, Hannah wondered how often they needed to replace it. Jones handed the bed net to Hannah.

Hannah handed the bed net to Wilkister and hugged her. "Bye, Wilkister!"

"Oh, thank you, Hannah. Thank you, Mrs. Higgins. Thank you, Jones." *They'll all have to pile into one bed. We should have gotten more.*

"We can get more," Hannah winced.

"No, no," Wilkister said. "One for family is good. We share in one bed." *Everyone in one bed? You, Evelyn, Dani, and your two brothers?*

Hannah's mom took a step inside and gave Wilkister a hug. Hannah caught her mom checking the place out and wondered what she was thinking. Jones patted Wilkister on the head. Dani came to the door. "This my dani."

They shook hands and thanked her. Nodding and smiling, Dani softly repeated, "Asante, asante." She understood English but did not know how to speak many words.

On the way home, Hannah asked about going to

Nairobi to meet with Sarah Oloo. She pleaded her case to get her mom to agree.

"I don't know, Hannah. A bus to Nairobi?" Her eyes looked sad.

"Please, Mom? Uncle Brian would be so happy."

She put her arm around Hannah. "He's already so happy with you. I know he is."

She nestled into her mom. "Wilkister and I just want to do something for him." She sat up. "And we could get her Sour Patch Kids. Remember?"

Jones interrupted. "Sour Patch what? Kids?" He looked alarmed.

Laughing, Hannah and her mom explained. Jones seemed relieved. And still a little confused.

"Can we think about it, Hannah? And I need to ask Dad."

"Dad?" she yelled. "Why do you need to ask Dad? He's not even here."

Her mom looked at her and lifted one eyebrow. She whispered through gritted teeth, "We'll think about it."

Quieting her voice, Hannah said, "Okay, but we need to go soon. Harvest Festival is next week. And then we're going home. It will be too late."

"We'll think about it," her mom repeated.

Hannah crossed her arms and harrumphed. *We'll think about it means we're not going.*

They arrived back at the Classic and Hannah hugged

Jones. He was leaving that night for Kitui. "Please tell Rebecca and Anthony I say hi!" She started toward the Classic and then turned back. She ran back to Jones and gave him another hug. "I'll really miss you."

He laughed. "I miss you too, Hannah." He hugged her extra tight. She smiled and waved goodbye as she ran inside to give Grace her bracelet.

Fever Sweat

Hannah woke up in the middle of the night to the sound of her mom coughing. She heard her try to breathe in, start to choke, and sit up. Reaching underneath the bed net, Hannah grabbed her water bottle from the table and handed it in to her mom. She bit her nails and breathed unsteadily as she watched her mother gulp the hot water. Hannah's mind raced. *I can't get you toast or ginger ale. We took the peanut butter crackers and protein bars to the clinic. Should I wake Grace up? Can I call Patrick and ask him to take us to the Nakumatt? Is the Nakumatt even open?*

Her mother felt her own forehead with her left hand. She reached for Hannah's forehead with her right hand. Hannah looked at her mom's pale and sweaty face. Different than the sweat from the climate in Kenya, this sweat was fever sweat. Resting next to her mom, Hannah's eyelids became heavy and she fell back to sleep.

Her mom was still sleeping when Hannah woke up, so she went downstairs. Weeping in the comfort of Grace's arms, Hannah told her how sick her mom was. Grace was wearing her bracelet. Hannah wiped her tears away and explained. "I've been saying things like, 'You're just nervous. You're using being tired as an excuse.'" Hannah looked into Grace's eyes. "And I think she's really sick."

"Is okay, sweet Hannah. Is all okay." Grace held her. "I make tea for your mum. You want stay in Kisumu today? Hector come back to ICRAF today from Nairobi."

Hannah nodded. "But Wilkister thinks we might be going to Nairobi. And now we're not. And I can't call her and tell her." She sniffed.

"Is okay. Jones leave for Kitui already, but I call Patrick, he call Dr. Omundo..."

Hannah finished the trail. "And Dr. Omundo can tell Kiano's mom and she can tell Kiano and Kiano can tell Wilkister. Sheesh, that's a lot of people for one message."

Grace nodded. "We manage."

Hannah hugged her again.

"Grace?"

"Yah, Hannah," she responded, her arm around Hannah as they walked to the kitchen to make tea.

"Can we go to the Nakumatt to get my mom some crackers and ginger ale?"

"Is OK, yah. I do no know ginger ale, but we go to Nakumatt today and you choose for your mum. And we go to ICRAF to see Hector, too. Is big day today. But let first go check to your mum."

They walked upstairs and quietly opened the door. Watching her mom sleep with heavy breathing caused tears to well up in Hannah's eyes. The sight of her pale, glistening mom sleeping under a smelly bed net in the intense heat upset her. By the time she would get the ginger ale back to her—if the Nakumatt even had ginger ale—it would be hot. She thought of Wilkister and the people at the clinic. The stillness of the heat and the stench in the air was even thicker out in Sauri. *They must get so uncomfortable. And they take only what they need.*

"Let Mum sleep. We go to ICRAF first or to the Nakumatt? You choose, sweet Hannah," Grace whispered as they walked out of the room and back down the stairs.

"Nakumatt, please," she answered. "We can come back, check on my mom and see if she wants crackers or ginger ale and see what else she needs, and then we'll go to ICRAF to see Hector. Is that good?"

"Yes, is okay. But is what ginger ale?"

They took boda-bodas several kilometers on the back of creaky bikes, with the riders laboring through the rough terrain of the paths, dodging potholes and ditches. Hannah thought of Brian on the boda-boda and smiled. She thought of her mom sleeping next to Beary and felt comfort in all of their new friends in Kisumu and Sauri taking such good care of them. She thought of Livvy and how much she would love Ash. And then she thought of her dad. They pedaled over a bump and Hannah grabbed on to the back of the African boy steering the bike. "I sorry," she heard him say softly.

"That's okay," she said and he kept on pedaling.

Her thoughts went back to her dad. *I wish he was here.* She shrugged.

They arrived at the Nakumatt and Hannah reached into her little purse, navy blue with a pink elephant, just big enough to hold cash. The young men on the bikes told her how much she owed them, 40 bob total, about sixty cents. "US dollar?" they asked.

"You would rather have a US dollar?"

"Yes, yes," they said, nodding their heads and smiling.

She looked at Grace and smiled. She reached into her elephant purse, hoping she had an American dollar bill. She had two! She handed each of them one bill. They high-fived holding the dollars and pedaled off saying, "US dollar!"

Grace and Hannah smiled and watched them ride away.

The Nakumatt did not have saltines, but it did have plain flat biscuits. Hannah got two packs. Surveying the drink options, she saw bottled water and an orange drink that was neither soda nor orange juice, somewhere in between. There was not any ginger ale, so Hannah got bottled water and two orange drinks.

"Do you want anything, Grace?" she asked.

"No, no," Grace answered.

"Are you sure? You bought everything last time."

"Yes, yes, I sure, thank you, Hannah."

Moving swiftly up and down each aisle, Hannah searched for candy that resembled Sour Patch Kids. She could not find anything. *Oh, well. We're probably not going anyway. Even if Mom gets better soon.*

Carrying everything back on boda-bodas, they walked upstairs quietly and looked in on her mom who was still sleeping. Hannah tiptoed closer to her. She could hear her mom breathing steadily. And Beary seemed to be on guard, watching over her, protecting her. Feeling better herself, Hannah giggled softly. *She's in good hands with Beary.* She left the biscuits and orange drink by her mom's bed so she would see them if she woke up while she and Grace were at the ICRAF Center.

Grace insisted Hannah eat before going to ICRAF. Hannah agreed and ate some bread while Grace made her hot tea. Despite the intense heat, there was something very soothing about hot tea and Grace's company. Hannah felt safe with her.

"You are worried to your mum, yes?" Grace asked as she poured the hot water into a tin cup for Hannah.

"Yes," Hannah answered. *Should I call my dad? What could he do?*

"Ah, is good," Grace said. "She be okay, yes."

Hannah smiled and took a sip of her tea.

They walked together to the ICRAF Center where Hector was working. "Allo?" Grace called out as they walked in.

"Jambo!" boomed Hector as he walked toward them, smiling. "Jambo, Grace," he said and shook her hand and then Hannah's. "And jambo and asante to you, little Hannah." She giggled. She was almost the same height as he was.

"Jambo, Hector," she answered. "But why are you thanking me? Why did you say, 'Asante'?"

He laughed and hugged her. "I'll tell you. Come sit down."

The three of them walked into the room with the clunky computers and sat down on the ripped vinyl chairs at the table in the center. The air was so humid that even though she was wearing long pants, Hannah felt stuck to the vinyl seat.

"I was in Nairobi for the last few days at agriculture meetings with government officials." Hannah and Grace nodded and he continued talking. "And the office assistant said there was a message for me—a request for a meeting that had not been scheduled." He looked into Hannah's eyes, smiled and asked, "And guess who called that meeting?"

Hannah thought about it for a minute. She knew meetings in government agencies frustrated her Uncle Brian because it took forever to move forward on projects. She remembered his focus on progress even in the most exasperating moments.

"Who?"

"Sarah Oloo!" he responded and laughed with delight.

"Sarah Oloo? Really? She asked for a meeting with you? What did she say?" Suctioned on the chair, her skin snapped when she jumped up. She rubbed the backs of her thighs and laughed.

"She asked about you."

Hannah froze. "About me?"

"She said she met you on her way to Kisumu the other week and she had not stopped thinking about you. And she was very sorry to hear about Brian when I told her." He bowed his head.

"I can't believe she remembered us! Why was she thinking about us? What else did she say?"

"She said she wants to come out to Sauri sometime soon."

"She did? She wants to come out to Sauri? When? What day? Can it be before my mom and I leave? We can meet her anytime she wants!" Hannah's smile had become as large and lasting as those of her new Kenyan friends.

"Well," he said, "I tried to schedule an exact date and time, and she was unable."

Deflated, Hannah asked, "What do you mean she was unable? What does that mean?"

"She will come," he said with confidence and pride.

"But she didn't set a date and time. And we're leaving next week." Hannah groaned. She looked out the window into the dusty, hazy sky and thought of Uncle Brian. "Can we go see her?" Her voice cracked.

"Go see Sarah Oloo? In Nairobi?" He looked at Grace who tilted her head to the side waiting for his response.

"I can call her and ask to see her." Hannah offered and gulped. *Mom is going to be really mad.*

Hector smiled. "You can try." He reached into his wallet and handed Hannah a business card with Sarah Oloo's contact information. *Jackpot!*

"What did you talk about in your agriculture meetings, Hector?" she asked.

"Irrigation systems, soil, seed, crops. We talked about dry land and how to use funding efficiently to get the most food to the most people."

Hannah nodded. "Oh," she said. "We studied science yesterday and the teacher talked about weather, soil, seed, measurements, markets, and all that stuff. What about planting a small harvest at Bar Sauri Primary?"

Hector looked at her, his left eyebrow raised a little higher than his right. "What do you mean?"

"There are these things at home called edible schoolyards. I don't know much about them, but I think kids grow small crops at school and learn about science and math, and they get to eat the fruits and vegetables they plant."

Hector's jaw dropped and his brown eyes widened.

"And what about the community food program Uncle Brian and his friends started? Can some of that food be used at the school so kids can have nyoyo for lunch every day?" As Hannah shared her idea, she wondered if there was enough maize and beans at the flour mill to feed the kids at school and still have enough for everyone else. *Take only what you need. Leave what you can.*

"Nyoyo at school every day," Hector repeated. He looked at Hannah. "People were waiting for you with great expectations. And you are giving them all they hoped for, Hannah," he said proudly. "And more."

Hannah smiled. "It was Wilkister's idea to meet with Sarah Oloo." She looked out the window toward the Classic. "And all of you sure have done a lot for us."

Grace noticed Hannah staring out the window. "You two are talk more. I go check on mum, is good?"

Hannah told Grace she would rather go back with her. Grace assured Hannah that her mom would probably still be sleeping and promised she would call Hector when her mom woke up. She said Hannah should spend time with Hector while he was there and since there was Internet connection that day. "And then you come home soon. Hector bring you."

Hannah nodded and Grace walked out the door.

"Give a man a fish and he eats for a day. Teach him to fish and he eats for a lifetime," Hector said and smiled.

"You're teaching me how to fish," Hannah answered.

"We teach each other how to fish," Hector said.

Hector returned Hannah to the Classic later that afternoon, and Grace reported that Hannah's mom was still sleeping. "I think we should wake her up, right? Did she eat anything?"

"No, no," Grace said. "She eat and drink nothing. I think you right. We wake her." Hector said to call him if they needed anything and Hannah and Grace went upstairs.

Hannah walked toward the bed and lifted the bed net. "Mom?" she whispered. "Mom?" She gave her a little nudge. She nudged her again, a little harder.

Her mom shifted the littlest bit and tried to open her eyes. They were crusted together, and her lids seemed very heavy. Reaching her arm over to rub her eyes, she seemed to be laboring to move at all. Hannah gasped. Her mom looked just like the man at the clinic with the sunken yellow eyes, the man who had turned out to be Kiano's uncle, the man who had died.

"Mom!" she called out. "Are you okay?" Her skin was so pale and she was sweating profusely.

"Water. Please."

Hannah got the fresh water bottle from the Nakumatt.

She took the cap off and passed it to her mom. Her mom sat up a bit and started drinking. She took a few sips and then put it back down.

"I got you an orange drink and biscuits at the Nakumatt, Mom. Do you want that?"

She shook her head no.

"Well, you have to have something, Mom. And I need to call Dad."

Grace said, "I get bread and hot tea. Is good to her."

"You need to eat something, Mom. How about a biscuit?" Grace hustled in with the bread. She was out of breath. Hannah helped her mom sit up and take a sip of water. Breaking a piece of bread, she handed it to her mom, who took a bite and put her head back down. Hannah opened the package of biscuits and broke off a piece for her mom, who waved it away. She closed her eyes and went back to sleep.

Hannah looked up at Grace with tears in her eyes. "Is okay, Hannah," Grace said. "We take tea downstairs now. She be okay."

Telling Dad

As they drank their tea, Hannah tried to get her mind off her sick mom.

"Your mum be okay, is okay," Grace said, and touched Hannah's forearm.

"I just wish my dad was here," she confided. "He could help take care of my mom." She paused. "And me." She looked away.

"We here take care of you, Hannah. We take care of your mum, too."

"No, no, I know," she said. "You've been so good to both of us." She looked up at Grace and smiled. Then she looked down at her lap again. "It's just that my dad isn't here."

"Ah," Grace nodded her head.

"Why didn't he just come with us in the first place?" She started to cry. "I just want him here. I want him to *want* to be here. He said he wished he had come with us."

Grace moved her chair closer to Hannah so she could put her arm around her. "Maybe you call your dad?" She suggested.

Hannah knew she had to call her dad and tell him about her mom. *Maybe that will get him to come.* "Last time I talked to him, he was upset he didn't come with us. And now my mom is sick." Slumping up the stairs and into the bedroom, she reached into her mom's bag and got the cell phone. She walked outside and sat on the stairs.

The phone rang a few times. She heard his voice, "Meredith?"

"Hi, Dad. It's me."

"Oh, hi Han. How are you?"

"Well," she stammered, "I, uh..."

"What's wrong?"

His panicked voice made Hannah even more nervous and she started to cry.

"Hannah! What is it?"

"It's just," she paused. "Everything is fine. It's just... It's just that I wanted to say, 'I love you.'"

He let out a loud breath. "You're sure you're all right? And Mom's okay?"

"Uh huh, I'm sure."

"Okay," he said. "I love you, too, Hannah. Did you call

to tell me something else, though? And where's Mom?"

"She's sleeping. She is a little sick, but Grace said she'll be okay."

"Awww, no," he shrugged. "I knew something would happen."

"I didn't want to tell you."

"You guys have to come home." He moaned. "Please have Mom call me when she gets up—even if it's the middle of the night your time or my time—just have her call me, okay? And if she gets worse…" He stopped. "Just have her call me."

"Okay, Dad."

"And you're okay? You're sure?"

"Yes, I'm fine."

"I love you, Hannah."

"I love you, too, Dad."

Hannah walked back into the room she shared with her mom. She put the phone back in her mom's bag and sat on the floor. Her mom still slept.

She walked downstairs and Grace was sitting outside. "Hannah," she asked. "How it went with your dad? Is all okay?"

"Yeah, he's worried about my mom, but you're sure she'll be fine, right?"

Grace nodded and pointed toward Ash, who was sleeping on the porch. Hannah walked over and sat down next to her furry friend. Shifting her weight to protect her skin and clothes from the splintery wooden panels, she leaned into Ash. She rested her head against his body and he wagged his tail.

"Hannah? Hannah?" Grace nudged her. "Your mum, she is awake, Hannah. You want see her?"

Hannah had fallen asleep with Ash as her pillow. Having no idea what time it was, she yelled, "Yes!" and gave Ash a kiss on the top of his head. She got up and ran upstairs to her room.

"Mom." She went over to her mom's side of the bed. She lifted the bed net and saw her mom's droopy open eyes and weak smile. "Hi," she whispered. She handed her the orange drink and the packet of biscuits.

"No, that's okay, thank you. Grace is getting me some bread and hot tea."

Hannah smiled and asked, "How are you feeling?"

She nodded her head and answered simply, "Better." She took a deep breath and propped herself up. "Much better."

Hannah went to the other side of the bed and crawled in beside her. She moved Beary so she was in the middle and he was on the end.

"I talked to Dad earlier and he asked me to have you call him, no matter what time it was."

Grace walked in with the hot tea and bread. Hannah got up to get the phone.

"We have banana and orange, too. I go get for you."

"Thank you, Grace."

Hannah continued talking as her mom took a sip of the hot tea. "He's sad he's not here. And he thinks it's too late to come now." She put Beary on her lap and sat next to her mom. "He said he wishes he had been here because he would have spent more time with Uncle Brian." Tears fell from her cheeks onto Beary.

With one arm around Hannah, her mom took another sip of tea and put the cup down on the floor beside the bed. She broke off a piece of bread and ate it. Grace walked in with a banana and an orange. "Thank you, Grace," Hannah's mom said. "Would you sit with us for a while?"

"Yes, sure," Grace answered and sat down on the wooden chair in the corner of the room. Ash nudged the door open and walked in. "Ash!" she called out, and then spoke in Swahili. Hannah thought of Livvy learning Swahili and decided to teach Ash more English. She sat up in bed, wiped the tears from her eyes and giggled.

"No, he's okay here," Hannah insisted. He trotted over to Hannah's side of the bed and curled up on the floor.

"Do you want the orange or the banana, Mom?"

"I'll have the orange, please. And I am just going to call Dad quickly to let him know everything is fine. Grace, please stay. I'll just be a minute."

Hannah peeled the orange while her mom spoke briefly to Hannah's dad and assured him she was all right.

Hannah and Grace told her mom about the school lunch program and the edible schoolyard ideas while she ate the orange. Ash slept beside them.

A Chance to Do Something Good

Hannah stayed in Kisumu the next few days to take care of her mom, and the following morning she woke up to a familiar voice she heard talking with Grace outside. "Jones!" she called out and ran downstairs.

"Hannah! There you are! I have surprise for you." He had his hands behind his back.

"A surprise? For me? What is it?"

He laughed and opened his hand to reveal her treat.

"No way!" She screamed. "Sour Patch Kids!" Hugging him, she clutched the pack in her fist. "Where did you find them?"

"At bus station stop in Nairobi on way to Kitui." He smiled and put his arm around her. "I know they have there because Brian, when he call to tell me what bus he on, he say he got your favorite candy for you at Nairobi bus station. He was so happy he found for you. And when you say Sour Patch Kids, I remember."

Bursting into tears, Hannah hugged Jones. "Thank you," she said.

Grace put her hand on Hannah's back. "How is your mum this morning, Hannah?"

"She's still sleeping. Should I go wake her up?"

"Yes, I think is good idea."

Hannah raced upstairs. Ash trotted behind her. "Mom?"

Her mom moved and moaned. She opened her eyes, yawned and stretched her arms above her head into the bed net. "Hi," she said softly. "What time is it?"

Hannah picked up her phone. "10 a.m."

Sitting up and smiling, her mom asked, "Jones is back? He's downstairs?" She swung her legs around the side of the bed.

"Whoa, hang on. What are you doing, Mom?"

"I want to go see him. He's downstairs with Grace?" She picked up a pile of medical papers by her bed. She had been tracking medicine in and out of the clinic, numbers of people treated and numbers of deaths. "I need to finish these," she said weakly. "This information will help get more funding to the clinic for more medicine and maybe even another doctor."

"You sure are feeling better," Hannah said, still a little worried.

Her mom nodded. "I'll get to them this afternoon. Come on." She grabbed Hannah's hand. "Let's go see Jones and hear about his trip."

Jones got teary telling about his time with Rebecca and Anthony. He missed them so much already. Happy to hear about plans for the school lunch program and edible school yards, Jones asked if they had made a plan to go to Nairobi and meet with Sarah Oloo.

Hannah looked up at her mom. "Um," she said. "While you were sleeping yesterday, Hector gave me her business card. He said she remembered us, Mom. Can I call her today? And just see what she says?" Her mom looked at her and sighed. "Please?" she asked.

"Okay, you can call her. But that doesn't mean we're going." Hannah dashed upstairs to get Sarah Oloo's contact card and the phone. She could hear her mom's voice calling behind her. "Did you hear me, Hannah? It doesn't mean we're going."

She returned to the table and dialed the number. Her heart raced.

"Allo? Office to Sarah Oloo."

"Hi, my name is Hannah Higgins. May I please speak to Ms. Oloo?" Her voice trembled.

"Is who?"

"Hannah Higgins. I met her in Kisumu a few weeks ago."

"And is about what?"

Hannah panicked. She bit her lower lip. Her eyes darted left to right. Putting her hand over the phone, she leaned into her mom. "She wants to know what I want to talk to her about."

"Is road construction, yah?" Grace said.

"Yes!" Hannah put the phone back up to her face. "Road construction," she said.

"She have to call you back."

"Oh, okay." As Hannah was in the middle of leaving her phone number, the woman thanked her and hung up the phone.

Hannah sighed. Her shoulders shrugged. Her bottom lip quivered. "She didn't even wait for my phone number."

Hector walked up behind her. "Then you call again," he said. "She has a big job, Sarah Oloo."

"You sound like you're making excuses for her, Hector," Hannah's mom responded.

"No, Meredith, please," he said. "The government regulations challenge its employees, and some of the employees are not good, but there are some who are. I think Sarah Oloo is good."

"Then I'll call her again tomorrow," Hannah agreed.

He put his hand on her shoulder. "You call her again today."

Hannah looked up at him. "Okay," she agreed and smiled. "I'll call her again today." Thinking about leaving in five days and with Harvest Festival coming up, Hannah looked at her mom. "If we're going to go to Nairobi, we really have to go tomorrow. Don't we?" *This is our chance, Mom. To do something good.* "Please, Mom? Please?"

Her mom looked up at Grace, Hector, and Jones. They all nodded.

"Okay, Hannah. We can go."

Hannah cheered. "And can we take Wilkister?"

"No, Hannah. We can't take Wilkister."

Hector added, "I will go out to Sauri to make preparations for Harvest Festival. Wilkister can help me."

Hannah pursed her lips. "But it was her idea to make the roads better for Uncle Brian. If anyone gets to go, it should be her." She sat down and crossed her arms.

Hannah's mom sighed and looked at Jones. He laughed. "Is okay, yes. I get Wilkister in the morning. And we go to Nairobi."

"Her grandmother said she could go, but how will she know we're coming? How will she know to be ready?"

Jones winked. "Rooster crows at 5 a.m. She be ready."

Mirror in Nairobi

When Wilkister pulled in to the Classic Guest House in the truck with Jones, Hannah cheered. *What an adventure!*

"Have you been to Kisumu before?"

"No, no," she said as she climbed out of the truck and looked around. Her eyes widened and her mouth hung open. "Is so big here." *What would she think of New York City? What will she think of Nairobi?* "I never go on bus before, Hannah." She grabbed Hannah's hands. "I so excited!"

"Me too!" Hannah exclaimed. She had not reached Sarah Oloo, but that would not stop her. Hannah knew this is what her Uncle Brian would have done.

Patrick reviewed the schedule with Hannah's mom. Hannah listened in. "You will meet driver at Nairobi bus station. He take you to the Intercontinental Hotel."

Intercontinental Hotel. That was forever ago. "Next morning at 6 a.m., driver meet you at hotel and take you to Sarah Oloo's office. He wait for you and take you back to bus station, okay? You never walk alone."

"Thank you so much, Patrick." Her mom hugged him and took the paperwork with her. Hannah sighed a breath of relief, hugged Patrick, and got in the truck with Jones, her mom, and Wilkister.

When they arrived, there was not much at the bus station, not even a bus. Hannah looked around. "Are we in the right place?" Jones assured her they were and that he would stay with them until the bus arrived. It was scheduled to leave at 7:30 a.m. It was 7:25 a.m. No one was there. *I don't think I'll ever get used to Africa time.*

"I'm sorry, Mom. Remember when we first got here? I called you frantic for worrying. I'm sorry I made fun of you." She leaned in and whispered. "And I'm the same way. I can't believe the bus isn't even here yet."

"That's okay, Hannah."

The bus pulled in and people flooded the station. *Where did all these people come from?* Hannah hustled out of the truck worried they would not get seats. Realizing she had forgotten to say bye to Jones, she raced back and hugged him through the open window. "Thanks, Jones."

"Good luck, Hannah. You do good." He gave her a thumbs up.

She waved to him and ran back to meet her mom and

Wilkister, who were standing in line. They bought tickets and got on the bus. Hannah and Wilkister sat next to each other. Her mom sat behind them.

Hannah had been on a bus before, so she let Wilkister have the window seat. She put her elbow on the armrest and propped her head up with her hand. When she woke up three hours later, Wilkister was in the same position staring out the window. She hardly blinked. Hannah took off her glasses and rubbed her eyes. Sitting up on her knees, she turned around and saw her mom sleeping. She cringed as she watched her mom's head bang against the window with every bump. She looked out over Wilkister's head. The landscape had become textured with shades of green and brown. There were more trees. She looked ahead through the windshield. The roads had become more uniform. There were even two lanes. She sat back down in her seat and wondered where along the road Uncle Brian's bus had flipped and then decided she would rather not know.

"You think we see animals, Hannah?" Wilkister asked.

Hannah shrugged her shoulders. "I don't know." She looked over Wilkister's head out the window. "I don't think so. We're getting closer to the city. The animals are in the safaris, aren't they?"

Wilksiter turned and looked at her. "Yah, you are

right. I hope we see lion."

Hannah laughed.

"What is funny?"

"I don't know," Hannah said. "You live in Africa and you've never seen a lion."

"You think every African see lions?"

Hannah's cheeks blushed. "No." She scratched her head. "Well, maybe. I don't know. It's just when I think of Africa, I think of safari animals. But you're right, I've only seen cows, chickens, goats, and dogs."

"And my rooster!"

Hannah laughed again. "And your rooster. And some lizards. And that thing that was not a beetle."

Wilkister giggled.

"What do you see when you think of America?" Hannah asked. "Not safari animals."

"No," Wilksiter agreed. "Not safari animals." She looked out the window to the horizon. "I do not know. I never see anything about America." Turning her body back to Hannah, she said, "But I know you and your mum. And Brian. And I think people in America are good."

Unsure of what to say, Hannah responded. "A lot of people in America are good, that's true. A lot of people here are good, too, Wilkister. My mom and I love it here. And you know my Uncle Brian did, too."

Wilkister took Hannah's hand and looked back out

the window. *What would I want her to know about America? Why did I assume she's seen a lion? There aren't lions in Sauri... are there?*

"Hannah?" Her mom woke her up. Wilkister slept beside her. "We're almost here. Help me look for the driver and we'll go to the hotel. You can call Sarah Oloo's office once we get there. She might have left for the day but we can try."

Straightening her glasses, Hannah nodded. She nudged Wilkister and grabbed her bag. She had not noticed Wilkister did not have one. "Mom," she whispered. "Wilkister didn't bring a bag."

"I know. I've got it, don't worry."

Wilkister stepped off the bus and looked around. Remembering her feeling of being lost in Times Square when she first arrived in Nairobi, Hannah looked at Wilkister spinning slowly in place, her eyes gazing upward.

There was a man with a sign marked HIGGINS. They walked up to him and got in the car.

Checking into the Intercontinental Hotel, Hannah looked around. Everything about it seemed luxurious—the bright lights, the paintings on the walls, the shiny countertops. Everything sparkled. They walked to their room.

"You want to take a shower first, Wilkister?"

Looking down at the ground, Wilkister shook her

head.

"Okay, I'll go first!" Hannah squealed.

She took a shower with hot water, shampoo and soap. The water pressure massaged the top of her head and removed days of dirt from her hair and body. She wore a bathrobe that was soft and smooth against her clean skin. Her hair glistened and smelled fresh. She walked back out to the bedroom and turned on the TV. The colors on the screen overwhelmed her. They seemed so bright. Almost in a trance, she caught herself with her mouth wide open and felt a little drool coming out its side. Wiping the drool with the back of her hand, she climbed into the bed and nestled under a blanket and a comforter. The pillow was so fluffy. The air conditioning kicked in. Wilkister remained seated at the edge of the bed in her purple dress.

"It's your turn, Wilkister. I'm going to call Sarah Oloo." She dialed.

"Allo?"

"Hi! May I please speak to Sarah Oloo?"

"Yes, this Sarah Oloo."

Hannah gulped. "She's on the phone!" Her mom came running from the bathroom. Wilkister stayed seated.

"Hi, Ms. Oloo. My name is Hannah Higgins. I met you on the plane from Nairobi to Kisumu about three weeks ago." There was silence on the other end. "You met with Hector Sanchez the other day." She let out a breath. Still nothing. "You met my uncle before. About building roads near Sauri."

"Ah, yes, Hannah. I remember. And I sorry about your uncle."

"Thank you." She gulped again. "I am in Nairobi and hope I can meet with you. Tomorrow morning?"

"Oh, no, no. I am very busy. Tomorrow is very busy."

Hannah got up and paced around the hotel room. "But I'm only here tomorrow. And I just wanted to talk with you for five minutes. I promise."

Hearing a heavy sigh on the other end of the phone, Hannah held her breath. She bit her upper lip and waited.

"Okay, five minutes. I see you at 8 a.m. for five minutes."

"Yes! Okay! 8 a.m. I'll see you tomorrow."

"You know where is my office?"

"Yes! I know. Thank you so much, Ms. Oloo! I'll see you tomorrow."

"See you tomorrow, Hannah. And please. Call me Sarah."

"Thank you, Sarah! Asante!"

She heard laughter. "Karibu sana, Hannah. Bye."

"Bye!"

She high-fived her mom. "We did it!" She went to high-five Wilkister, who was still sitting at the edge of the bed. "What's wrong?" She sat down next to her.

"I've got it," Hannah's mom whispered and patted her on the knees as she walked with Wilkister into the bathroom. *I'm such an idiot. Wilkister probably doesn't know how the shower knobs work. And has she seen a TV? Does she know what air conditioning is? People have taken me around everywhere since I got here. They've answered my questions. I've never been left alone. Not for a minute.* She got up and poked her head into the bathroom.

"I'm sorry, Kister. I wasn't thinking."

Wilkister was smiling like the Cheshire Cat. "No, I good! I going to take a shower!"

Hannah giggled. She and her mom listened to make sure everything was okay and they heard Wilkister singing. Hannah chimed in from the bedroom. Swing Swing. Her new favorite song.

Wilkister changed out of her purple dress into a t-shirt and pajama bottoms Hannah's mom had brought. "Just like you, Hannah!" Feeling like she finally had a little sister, Hannah shined. With two double beds in the room, they offered Wilkister her own bed. She frowned. "I never sleep by myself before. Is okay I sleep with you? We all sleep together?"

"I can sleep with you, Wilkister, and my mom can sleep in the other bed."

"We all sleep together?" She asked again.

Hannah and her mom laughed. "Yes!" Her mom said. "We can all sleep together. I just need to take a shower."

Hannah flipped through the TV channels. Stations were staticky. She did not recognize any of the programs.

"Do you know TV?"

"Yes, yes," she answered. "I see football game on TV one time. I know. And Kiano tell me about Mon Ami Club."

"Oh right," Hannah said. She walked over to the air conditioning. "Do you know air conditioning?"

"No."

"It keeps the air cool when it gets hot."

"Why?"

"In case it's too hot."

"Why?"

"Don't you ever get too hot?"

"Yes, and I drink water." She walked over next to Hannah and put her hand over the unit. "But this feel nice. Is good air conditioning."

"It sure is!"

Wilkister walked back to the bed like a zombie and stared at the TV. Hannah watched her and realized Wilkister was looking behind the TV into the mirror. She just about pressed her nose to it. Touching her face and moving her head from side to side, Wilkister examined herself. She took a step back and surveyed her full frame. Tilting her head to one side, she moved closer again and massaged the skin on her face—pushing up and down against her cheekbones and across her forehead, down one side, along her chin and back up the other side.

"What are you doing?" Hannah asked.

Wilkister said nothing.

Hannah walked up next to her and looked at her in the mirror. "Wilkister, what are you doing to your face?"

"I not see before. This my face." She touched her cheeks and moved her fingers along her face the way a blind person sees someone for the first time.

"You've never seen yourself? What do you mean?" Hannah's mind raced. *How is it possible she hasn't seen herself before? No mirrors. No clean water to see her reflection. What do I say to her?* "I'm glad you're finally getting to see yourself, Wilkister," she said. "Because now you know how pretty you are." She put her arm around her and they looked at each other in the mirror.

"You are pretty, too, Hannah." She smiled.

That night, Wilkister snored under a blanket between Hannah and her mom, who both giggled on either side of her until they fell asleep.

Elevators and Roller Coasters

"What are you, the rooster?" Hannah asked when Wilkister woke her up at 5 a.m. the following morning.

"I sorry."

Hannah laughed. "No, that's okay." She grabbed a notepad and pen from the bedside table. "Let's think about what we're going to say to Sarah Oloo. I'll take notes."

"We say too many accident."

"Because of no roads," Hannah added.

Still in bed, her mom chimed in. "We can't say there are no roads, Hannah. There are roads. They're insufficient." She emphasized "insufficient".

Hannah crossed out "no roads" and wrote "insufficient road construction".

"Accidents could be prevented with sufficient roads? Is that good?" Hannah asked. Wilkister nodded.

"Do we say about Brian? We want memory to him?"

Hannah cringed. "I don't know. He never wanted it to be about him. He wanted it to be about the projects and the progress. What do you think?"

"I think memory to him is good."

"Mom, what do you think?"

She smiled. "I agree with Wilkister."

The driver was waiting for them downstairs. Still feeling so clean, Hannah got into the car with her mom and Wilkister and they drove to Sarah Oloo's office. Hannah had not seen Nairobi during the daytime. It was a lot like New York City—crowded with lots of tall buildings and restaurants. She did not feel so far away from home after all. As the driver pulled up to the office building, he told them he would circle around until they were finished and to wait right inside until they saw him. *Maybe I am far away from home after all.*

They walked into the building. Sarah Oloo's office was on the 20th floor. Wilkister looked up at the elevators and skipped a breath. "I wait here."

Hannah took her by the hand. Her mom took her other hand. "We will go together," Hannah's mom said. "You'll be okay, I promise."

Walking into the elevator, Hannah stood close to Wilkister, protecting her from the crowd of people. Wilkister took a step forward. "I okay." She smiled.

The first stop was the fourth floor. By the twentieth

floor, Wilkister was giddy. *She would love roller coasters.* Daydreaming about Wilkister visiting her, Hannah smiled. *Maybe one day.*

They announced themselves at the desk outside of Sarah Oloo's office. Hannah glowed. She looked out the window and thought of Uncle Brian. Wilkister walked over to the window and looked down. "Ugh!" She cried out and took a step back. Hannah giggled. *Maybe not roller coasters.*

After wiping the nervous sweat of her palms onto her skirt, Hannah shook Sarah Oloo's hand. "Thank you so much for having us." Sarah Oloo smiled and looked up at the clock. Hannah was reminded of her five-minute limit. "Do you remember my mom? And this is our friend, Wilkister." They all shook hands.

Hannah took the folded piece of hotel notepaper out of her little elephant purse. "We're here...uh." She stammered. Wiping her forehead, she continued. "We wanted to meet with you because...We're here."

Wilkister stepped forward. "My friend Brian Higgins die because no roads!" she blurted out.

Looking back down at her notes, Hannah pointed her index finger upward and said, "Insufficient road construction." Her stomach ached. She felt like she was letting her uncle down.

Sarah Oloo stood up behind her desk, walked around and stood between Hannah and Wilkister. Hannah's mom was standing to the side.

"Girls," Sarah Oloo said. "Thank you so much. And I am so sorry to your uncle and your friend." She looked up at Hannah's mom. "I am sorry."

"Harvest Festival is on Friday," Hannah said. "In Sauri. It's celebrating no one dying of hunger for a whole year."

Sarah Oloo tilted her head to the side and raised an eyebrow. "A whole year? Is good."

Hannah nodded. "It's really good because they are working together to stop hunger. We want to work together with you to end..." She looked down at her notepad. "Insufficient road construction."

Smiling, Sarah Oloo touched Hannah on the shoulder. "I know is insufficient. And is my job to make sufficient. I work for this, I promise."

"For my uncle?"

She nodded. "Yes, for your uncle."

"But what can you do?" Hannah wanted answers.

"I can keep working. We make more roads."

Not knowing what else to say, Hannah thanked her. She looked up at the clock. It had been more than five minutes.

They shook hands again and walked out. "Oh," Hannah said and reached into her pocket. "These are for you." She handed her the bag of Sour Patch Kids and walked out.

She melted into her mother's arms as they walked

to the elevator. "I don't know what I was expecting." she sobbed.

"She is working for Brian," Wilkister said. "That what we ask and that what she do. Is good meeting, Hannah." She patted Hannah on the back.

Hannah looked up at her and nodded. "Yeah, it was good, right?"

Her mom put an arm around each of the girls. "It was great," she insisted. "And I am proud of both of you."

Progress and Surprises

They slept the whole way back to Kisumu and crawled into bed as soon as they got back to the Classic. Wilkister and Hannah stayed together in Uncle Brian's room. Her mom slept in their room with Beary next to her.

Hannah woke up the following morning with Wilkister still sleeping beside her. She inched out of bed, put on her glasses and checked the time on her cell phone. 7:30 a.m. *The rooster would be shocked!* She giggled.

Closing the door behind her, she walked into her room and saw Beary alone under the bed net. "Where's my mom?" she whispered to Beary.

She walked downstairs and saw no one, not even Ash. Remembering being alone the morning she found out Uncle Brian had died, she was overcome with emotion and burst into tears. "Hannah! What is it?" Grace called out. She ran to Hannah and hugged her. Her mom hurried in behind Grace.

"Where were you?" Hannah yelled.

Her mom sat Hannah down on the porch steps. Ash jumped into her lap and licked the tears off her face. "What's the matter?" Her mom asked.

"I just didn't know where you were." Hannah cried.

Her mom hugged her. "I'm sorry, Hannah. I'm sorry."

Grace sat down on the other side of her and rubbed her back. "Me also," she added.

Feeling her cheeks burn, Hannah realized she had overreacted and apologized.

Grace broke the tension and announced, "We all sorry!"

Hannah wiped her face and giggled. "What were you doing at the ICRAF Center?" she asked, her breath beginning to steady.

Grace smiled and said, "There is surprise to you." Jones walked up and hushed Grace. Hannah's interest perked.

"A surprise?" She sniffed. "For me?"

Her mom laughed and said playfully, "Could be!"

"Seriously you guys. What's the surprise?"

Grace answered. "We serious no telling!"

Hannah giggled. *I love a surprise!*

Wilkister came downstairs. "Good morning! What we do today?"

Hannah looked at her mom who answered. "Jones and Hector are going to take us to the Nakumatt to get some things for Harvest Festival and then we'll go out to Sauri. You two will get to school a little late. Is that okay with you, Wilkister? What time is your dani expecting you back?"

"Is good. I tell her I be home today after school so is perfect."

On their way to the Nakumatt, Hannah told Hector and Jones about their meeting with Sarah Oloo.

"Ah," Hector said, his voice booming. "Great expectations have resulted in tremendous progress." He looked into her eyes. "Because of you." He looked at Wilkister. "And you." He reached his neck up to look over the girls and said to Hannah's mom, "And you, too." She smiled.

"You really think so?" Hannah asked. "I mean, we met with her and she promised she's working hard to build the roads, but nothing really happened in the meeting."

Hector chuckled. "Nothing really happened? What do you mean?" He threw his arms up in the air. "You had a meeting with a top government official in Kenya about the importance of road construction!" Hannah beamed. *Progress.*

They walked up and down the aisles looking for bowls, ladles, and large pots. Hector grabbed two pots from the shelves and put them in the cart.

"Hector?"

"Yes, Hannah?"

"There are bowls in the next aisle over. I'll go get them, but how many should I get? There are hundreds of kids. Not all of them go every day, but still, how many do you think we should buy?"

"Each child does not need a bowl. They can share," he answered. "So we get twenty. I'll bring the cart to you."

They bought all they needed to serve the food at school lunch and at Harvest Festival. Hannah looked down the aisle where she and Uncle Brian had talked and blew a kiss.

On the drive out to Sauri, Hannah took a seat next to Jones. She whispered, "I don't mean to be pushy, Jones, but what do you know about my surprise?"

Jones laughed aloud. "I know nothing of surprise. Is what surprise? For me?" He winked at her.

"No, it's for me," she answered, giggling. Then she looked at her mom and said, "Wait, is it for me?"

"I don't know what you're talking about, Hannah," her mom teased. "And neither does Jones."

"I do not know," Jones confirmed, stifling a giggle.

She said, "Harvest Festival is coming up soon. Does it have anything to do with that?" Neither of them said a word.

When they arrived in Sauri, Hector met with some of the teachers to create a schedule and figure out getting the maize and beans to the school, how the cooking would happen, how they might begin to determine quantities of food to cook and what they would do with the extra food each day. *Extra food.* There was no cafeteria or any food services employee, so they needed to work together to figure it all out. They would also begin to plan edible schoolyards for the next harvest season.

They pulled into the area in front of the flour mill. The loose beans were in a mound on the floor in a corner of the room without any covering at all. Ears of corn had been peeled and were piled on the floor in another corner. Flies swarmed like the ancient Roman army protecting its land and people. Irritated, Hannah smacked the flies away and realized in all the excitement of the beginnings of the school lunch program she had forgotten to spray DEET on her head that morning. She used DEET like hairspray. She shook her head around and swatted, but the flies were relentless.

Hector brought a canvas bag with him that he used to transport the loose beans and peeled ears of corn. They left some behind for people who might need them.

Hector took the bag filled with corn and beans and walked back to the school to talk more with the teachers while Jones drove Hannah's mom to the clinic. Patrick had stayed at the flour mill and would spend the day making preparations for the upcoming Harvest Festival. Hannah and Wilkister walked into the classroom. Mr. Awuor pulled them aside and caught them up on what they had missed. He asked about their meeting. As Hannah and Wilkister debriefed him, he asked them to share their experience with the class. The girls made an impromptu presentation and the kids craned their necks to get their ears close enough to hear every word. They especially loved what Wilkister had to say about the hotel. And having known Uncle Brian, they were all happy to hear about the attention to road construction. Kiano smiled the entire time.

Hannah got in a game of netball during morning recess. As she ran with the ball, dodged kids, and looked for someone open to pass to, her hair drove her crazy. Not only was it in her eyes—it was adhering to the sticky mixture of sweat and dirt on her face. She scanned the ground for her ponytail holder and did not see it. *Where did it go?* She passed the ball and then quickly brushed her hair behind her ears to stay in the game without missing a play. Within seconds it was back in her face. And it was hot and sticky against the back of her neck. *Ugh!* She looked around at the other girls. They all had shaved heads to keep the lice away. Her mom had been wearing her hair shorter for years, so she could not even hope to borrow a ponytail holder from her after school. She would have to wait until she got home that night.

Just before lunchtime, the kids were called out to a special assembly. Students followed the teachers out to a dirt field with two wicker chairs between two lone trees. Hannah looked around and thought of the auditorium where assemblies took place at her school. This setting was so much more peaceful. She could hear the sounds of goats, cows, chickens, and dogs, and even though smoke from burning trash and the stench in the air wafted straight under her nose as she breathed in, she loved it there.

Once the students were all seated on the ground, Mrs. Odhiambo put her index finger to her lips. As the students quieted, Hannah marveled at unspoken gestures that were universal—hugs, smiles, and even getting a big group of kids to be quiet. Hannah and Kiano sat next to each other with Wilkister just behind them. Hannah brushed her hair behind her ears and hoped it would just stick there with all the grime.

Mrs. Odhiambo announced that children were to continue to bring buckets of water to school, as many of them were already doing. She also asked the children to pick up large sticks on their way to school each morning. The kids looked at each other with confused expressions. Hannah giggled quietly. "What it is?" Kiano whispered to her. She shook her head that she was not going to tell. He asked Wilkister. She shook her head.

"We need water, and stick for fuel at our school because," she paused and looked around, increasing the anticipation among the children. "Because start tomorrow we have lunch for all children at school every day, is nyoyo!"

"We have nyoyo for lunch every day, Hannah! You can believe? Is so good." Kiano exclaimed.

Hannah looked at Kiano and smiled. "It is so good," she agreed.

That afternoon at school, the teacher gave an assignment to think of wishes. Hannah recognized this assignment from her school at home. She would always wish for another dog—a buddy for Livvy—and a room full of Sour Patch Kids. Now she would wish for medicine for Wilkister, jobs for the kids who finish secondary school, more beach balls and Frisbees, and a second netball hoop.

That night, Hannah reached into her toiletry bag for a hair tie and could not find any. She emptied it. Still nothing. She looked around the floor of her bathroom and the floor of their room.

Her mom who was already in bed reviewing the next order of supplies for the clinic poked her head through the bed net. "What are you looking for, Hannah?"

"I lost my ponytail elastic at school today and now I don't have any more."

"Oh, well, I am sure we can make a trip to the Nakumatt at some point soon." She went back to her papers.

"That's not even it," she snapped. Continuing her frantic search in her toiletry bag, around the small sink and along the floor, she said, "I just can't believe I've gone through an entire pack of hair ties. There were twenty of them in the pack, I know there were." She continued looking. "Did you know they put the beach balls and Frisbees in a shed for safekeeping and are only going to use them for special celebrations? Two beach balls and three Frisbees. And I can't keep track of even one hair tie."

"I understand, Hannah. It's late now. Finish washing up and come to bed. I'll braid your hair for now and we'll get you some at the Nakumatt and you can keep better track of those ones."

The kids out in Sauri are cheering that they'll get nyoyo at school, and I bring a whole pack of hair ties and can't hold on to even one of them.

She climbed in under the bed net and sat up facing away from her mom so she could start braiding her hair. She moved Beary over just a bit as she got situated, and there, under her little friend, was a blue hair tie. "Look at that," her mom said. "Beary had it the whole time." They both laughed. Hannah put her hair back in the blue hair tie, turned off the light, and went to sleep.

School Lunch

Hannah arrived to Sauri a little late the next morning, just as the bell was ringing to start school. The little boy she had given shillings to a week earlier ran up to her as she got out of the truck. "Hannah! Hannah!" he called to her. She waved bye to Jones and walked up to the boy who faced her with his arm extended. "This for you. I make for you." He handed her a hand carved wooden cell phone. Detailed with buttons and a screen, it looked just like the one Kiano had.

"Wow, Eliud!" she said. "This is awesome!" She put it up to her ear and said, "Allo?"

He reached into his pocket where he had another wooden cell phone. He put it up to his ear and said, "Allo!"

Hannah cracked up. "Allo, Eliud, this is Hannah. I

am calling to thank you so much for the super cool cell phone!"

"Ah," he answered, giggling. "You are welcome, Hannah. I hope you have good day to school today."

"You, too, Eliud. See you at school. Bye."

"Bye," he said, laughing. A few kids had gathered around and were laughing, too. Hannah put her arm around little Eliud as they walked into school. *I love it here.*

"Hannah," Wilkister said to her as she walked into the classroom. "It is going to be Harvest Festival, and then you are leaving."

"I know," Hannah responded. "I can't believe it." She looked down and tried not to think about it too hard.

"Can you come to sleep over with me? You can come Friday after school, we go together to my family, and you stay there? Then we go Saturday to Harvest Festival. Is okay?"

"Sure! I just have to ask my mom first, okay?"

"Sure, is good."

That day at school, they ended the class before lunch early. The kids had brought water in buckets on their heads and lots of big sticks to use for fuel. Hannah had not seen a body of water—even as small as a little creek—the whole time she had been there, but when Jones dropped her off a few mornings earlier, she had seen a little girl walking with a heavy bucket of water on her head. Hannah ran over to the girl and offered to carry the bucket the rest of the way to school. Afraid she would drop it if she carried it on her head, Hannah held the bucket in front of her, hunched over trying not to hurt her back or spill any. Hannah remembered stopping every few minutes to arch her back. Giggling, the little girl said, "Asante, Hannah."

They set up in the back of the school where there was a small fire pit in an enclosed area. When Hannah walked up to it, the smoke was already more than she could bear. Her eyes became irritated and red, and reminded her of adjusting to the intensity of the sun and dust when she first arrived.

Hannah circulated and took pictures of kids starting a fire in the fire pit by arranging sticks and rubbing them together. *I've only ever seen someone use a match.* She was convinced it was one of those things they made look very easy but was not—like Wilkister making necklaces and bracelets. She took pictures of kids pouring beans from Hector's canvas bag into the pot, roasting the maize, and scraping off the kernels into the pot of beans—another task they made look easy.

With every picture she took, the kids would rush to see. They would giggle and point and then get back to work preparing lunch.

Hannah noticed that the kids did not need to be shown how to prepare any of the food. And although the teachers were never too far away, there was hardly any teacher supervision at all. *There is no way we would be allowed to start fires at school.*

They scraped the corn off the cob with their fingers and used their hands to mix it together with the beans that were in the large pot. There must have been so much dirt mixed in with the corn and beans. Hannah remembered Uncle Brian's story about the worm. As long as it was cooked, it counted as protein. *What about the dirt and grime that was cooked?* She imagined Uncle Brian suggesting to think of it as a seasoning or a sauce and giggled.

The teachers made an announcement in Luo and all the kids formed a line. Hannah joined them. She put her phone down while they ate and thanked them for cooking while she took the pictures.

"Karibu sana," they answered.

Two teachers had large yellow buckets of water. The children walked forward and the teachers poured water over their dirty hands, which they rubbed together. They proceeded to another teacher who was serving the nyoyo with a ladle into a bowl. One bowl was given to every three children, who ate with their hands, each child reaching into the bowl again and again.

Small children would finish and take another helping. Big kids went back for seconds only after the little ones had eaten a second time. Teachers then took some for themselves and the nyoyo was gone.

Hannah, Wilkister and Kiano shared a bowl of the biggest beans and kernels of corn Hannah had ever seen. She inspected her hands to make sure her cuts from her fall had healed—hesitating for only a moment—and then began eating with her hands like the others. The nyoyo tasted delicious.

After they ate, Hannah took more pictures. The kids continued to scurry toward her with each picture she took. She thought of how funny it was that kids loved technology pretty much everywhere. *Kids loving technology is universal, too.* Then, one child asked, "Is me? This one, is me?"

Hannah looked at the photo and then at the little girl asking the question. "This one is you," she answered and pointed to the girl in the picture. The little girl said something in Luo and squealed with delight.

All the kids flooded her, "Is me? Is me? That is me?" they all asked.

Confused, Hannah started pointing out each child, even the older kids. *How do they not know which ones they are?* She thought back to Wilkister in the hotel room and it hit her like a ton of bricks. None of them had ever seen their reflections before. There were not any mirrors. The water the kids had brought in buckets had come from kilometers away—and it was murky, dirty and unclear.

She showed them their pictures as many times as they wanted—images of their happy, smiling faces.

After lunch, the teachers got out the beach balls and Frisbees to celebrate the special occasion of having lunch together that day, and to mark the beginning of a program that would give lunch to the kids at school every day. She watched as the children played with their new toys and started games of netball and football.

Wilkister called from the football game, "Hannah Banana, you play with us?"

"Sure!" Hannah called out and ran toward her friends.

Kiano and Hannah walked to the clinic together that afternoon after school. There was nothing to help with when they got there. The clinic was completely out of medicine and the line of patients was still long. Dr. Omundo wished Hannah and her mom, and Kiano and his mom, a good night and went back into the clinic to treat the next person in line as well as he possibly could.

On the drive back to Kisumu, they called Hector to tell him how well the first day of the school lunch program had gone, and then Hannah asked, "Mom? Can I sleep over at Wilkister's Friday night?"

"Oh," her mom said. She asked Jones what he thought.

He bobbed his head to the left and right. "I think not alone," he suggested.

"You think I stay with her?"

"Yes," he answered.

After dinner, Meredith and Hannah cleaned the dishes and talked with Grace about the day. Hannah told her all about the first day of the school lunch program and Grace kept saying, "Oh, Hannah, is good. Is very good." Hannah excused herself from post-dinner conversation with her mom and Grace to go upstairs and organize her things. She did not have much, but what she did have, she had managed to spread around to every square inch of the small room she had shared with her mom for almost a month.

It was Thursday evening. She was going to school on Friday and spending the night with Wilkister, then going to Harvest Festival on Saturday, back to Kisumu that evening and flying to Nairobi and then home.

As sad as she was to think about leaving, she was excited to see her dad and Livvy. It was the longest she had been away from both of them.

Sitting on the floor organizing her things, she looked up at the bed. Beary was propped up on her pillow underneath the bed net protected against malaria. Hannah laughed at him—her stuffed animal who had brought her so much comfort.

While brushing her teeth, she looked at the prescription bottles on the counter and realized it was the day of the week to take her antimalarial pill—to protect her against what Wilkister had. She took a swig of water from her water bottle and swallowed a pill. Her mom walked in the room.

"Mom, it's Thursday. You need to take your antimalarial pill."

Her mom laughed. "Funny you should mention it. I was coming up here to remind you the same thing."

As Hannah scrolled through the pictures on her

phone, she thought about the sleepover. She had been excited about it when Wilkister asked her, but she had started to get nervous.

"I'm glad you are coming with me to Wilkister's, Mom."

"What, Hannah? Wait," she said. "I'll be finished in a minute." She came out of the bathroom and climbed in under the bed net. "Now I'm ready. What were you saying?"

Hannah clutched on to Beary and started to cry. "What is it?" her mom asked in a gentle voice.

"I just feel bad. I feel bad they eat with their hands. I feel bad they don't have soap and eat with dirty hands. I feel bad that I checked to make sure my cuts were healed before I shared a bowl of food with Wilkister and Kiano. I feel bad they are so grateful to have nyoyo even though it has dirt and mud in it. I feel bad that my best friend out here asked me for a sleepover and I'm not sure I want to go. Why am I scared to go? She came all the way to Nairobi with us and I'm afraid to sleep at her house? What kind of friend does that make me?"

Her mom stroked the top of Hannah's head. Her hair was still tied back with the blue ponytail holder, which she had kept close track of that day. "I understand," her mom responded softly. "I feel the same way."

Hannah sat up a little and wiped the tears from her cheeks. "You do?"

"Of course I do," her mom said. "Every day at the clinic, I try hard not to breathe in fully because I am scared of getting sick again. These people—not just my patients, but also my new friends—are coming to me for care and help, and I am not even breathing in fully because I am worried about getting sick. And I feel bad there isn't enough medicine, but I feel even worse that I am grateful for the medicine I have, and even more for the medicine you have."

Hannah's eyes softened and she smiled. "You do understand," she said. She sat up a little more and moved Beary over. She spotted another hair tie. Orange. She laughed and said, "That scoundrel! He had two!"

Sleepover

Hannah packed her toothbrush, toothpaste, water bottle, and a clean pair of underwear. Her hair was tied back in a ponytail, still in the blue elastic. She was feeling less nervous about spending the night in Sauri, especially since her mom would be with her. She grabbed her backpack, zipped it up, and closed the door behind her.

On the way out to Sauri, Hannah listened to Jones and her mom talking about Jones driving back to Kisumu and getting in touch with Meredith throughout the day. "Why do you have to go back and forth to Kisumu today, Jones?" Hannah asked.

"Oh, just do things," he answered.

Hannah laughed and repeated, "Things? What kinds of things? For Harvest Festival?"

"Oh, yes." He looked at her and winked. "Is just things."

They arrived in Sauri early that morning. Jones dropped Meredith off at the clinic and then took Hannah to school. On their way, Hannah spotted Wilkister and her brothers walking along. Jones stopped the truck and as Hannah got out, she looked back at him and said, "Dropping me off here works well for you, since you seem to have a lot of driving to do today." She laughed and leaned back in through the open passenger window. "And Jones, thank you for the ride and for your help with whatever these surprises are."

"Is good, Hannah. Karibu sana," he said and waved as he drove away.

Hannah ran and caught up with Wilkister who was waiting for her. Wilkister's two brothers waved to her and then ran ahead.

"Hi, Kister."

"Jambo, Hannah."

"Did you already fetch the water?"

"No, my dani get it today. She take my sister for a walk to water since it is nice day today."

Hannah nodded. "Um, Wilkister?" She gulped. "Can my mom stay over with me?" Unable to imagine asking Emily if her mom could sleep over at her house, Hannah felt her cheeks blush. Tugging at the side of her long skirt, she hoped Wilkister would not think it was weird.

"Is okay, yah," she answered and smiled. "Your mum talk to my dani, is good."

"Thanks, Wilkister!"

That morning, the teachers called a special assembly. All the kids gathered in the assembly area—the same spot where they had learned about the school lunch program just a few days earlier. Mrs. Odhiambo and all the teachers stood up in front of the seated children and asked for volunteers to share their wishes. Hannah's heart raced. She wanted to share her wishes, but not in front of the whole school. She wanted to tell them how different her wishes had been before she got to Sauri and how they had changed. She wanted to thank them for their friendship.

Eliud raised his hand and was called up. He shared his wishes for festivals, for a bicycle for his family, for a cake for his upcoming birthday, and for Hannah to come back to Sauri. She looked up at him and he was looking out to her—in front of the whole school—with a big smile and huge tears in his eyes. Her heart melted.

More and more kids got up and shared their wishes. There were common themes of bicycles, birthday cakes, festivals, dancing, and for Hannah to return to Sauri. Some wished for medicine and for their parents to still be alive. Hannah took a deep breath and raised her hand.

She walked up to the front. Her knees wobbled. Her heart pounded. "We have this same assignment at home, and I usually wish for things for me." She heard her voice crack. "Like a bike, cake and dancing." She smiled. "And now I still wish for those things, and I also wish for medicine so that everyone is healthy, not just in Sauri, but in the world. I wish for all kids to have lunch at school and to be able to go to school." She looked to Mrs. Odhiambo and all of the teachers, and then out at all of the kids and said, "I wish everyone could have the chance to be part of this school and to be friends with all of you." She wiped tears from her cheeks and started walking back to her seat when Mrs. Odhiambo asked her to stay for a moment.

"Hannah," she said. "You hear the children all say they wish to you to stay here, to come back." She looked at the teachers and then to Hannah. "We wish is true, too. We want you come back, very soon." She reached behind her and picked up a basket. "Until you come back, we want you have basket to carry at home and think to us." Hannah looked at Wilkister and Kiano who were smiling. She thought of Brian's basket with green and purple trim and how he joked about carrying fruit on his head in New York City. She burst into tears. "Thank you," she said. "Asante sana." She hugged Mrs. Odhiambo and each of the teachers, and walked back to where she was seated.

After school that day, Wilkister, Hannah, and Kiano walked to the clinic. They waited while Meredith, Beatrice, and Dr. Omundo treated the remaining patients and then they wished Dr. Omundo a good night and navigated their way through the maize fields to Wilkister's hut.

When Wilkister's dani came out to greet her guests, she invited Beatrice and her family to join them for dinner and announced they were having a surprise meal. Forcing a smile, Hannah hoped whatever she had made tasted better than cow's meat. Beatrice accepted the offer and said she would bring kale from their crop.

By the time they arrived, it was already dark. Hannah could not see the moon or any stars. It was darker than a blackout at home. Wilkister's family had a gas lamp that Dani used to prepare the meal in the kitchen. The rest of the hut was dark. One of Wilkister's brothers suggested playing hide and seek. Hannah was relieved when Dani said that dinner was almost ready.

Dani asked everyone to sit at the table while she brought over a pot of food and the kale from Beatrice. Already on the table were a pitcher of water and a bowl. Wilkister got up from the table with the pitcher and the bowl. Everyone else remained seated and held out their hands. Wilkister poured water over each person's hands using the pitcher in her right hand and held the bowl with her left hand to catch the water. Hannah got up and helped hold the bowl as the amount of water increased and it became heavier. Wilkister thanked her and they continued around the table until everyone's hands had been washed. Then Wilkister and Hannah held the pitcher for each other and washed their own hands.

Dani had brought the gas lamp over to the table.

It was as if they had lost electricity and were eating by candlelight, but this was the way they ate every night. Hannah wondered if everyone had a gas lamp. Dani put food from the pot and kale on each plate and handed them down the table one by one. Hannah and her mom had brought their bottled water.

As she was about halfway through serving her guests, Dani announced proudly, "Is goat we have at dinner."

Hannah and her mom looked at each other. *Goat?* Hannah gulped.

Dani said a prayer before the meal. Hannah was glad it was dark so no one could see her full expression. Grossed out at the thought of eating goat, she could not imagine how it might taste. *If cow's meat was mostly bone and fat, what will goat taste like?* She cut a bit of goat and put some kale on her fork. She wished for maize. The kale would only make the goat taste bitter. She took a bite. It was chewy and she could not break it with her teeth. Trying not to gag, she quickly swallowed. The piece was too big and she coughed. She took her water bottle and drank. "You are okay, Hannah?" Wilkister asked.

"Yes," she insisted. "I was just eating it too fast." She looked over at Dani. "It's very good."

In the dim light, Hannah saw the silhouette of Dani's face. She was smiling.

After dinner, they sat around the table and talked. Hannah thought of how her family would typically sit together for dinner and talk, but sometimes they would watch TV. She liked talking and telling stories with her new friends without any distractions—except the chickens clucking outside.

Wilkister's family had a cow, so they had milk in their tea after dinner. The gas lamp was at the other end of the table, so Hannah could not see what she was drinking. She loved milk and had not had any since she had arrived in Sauri. She took a sip of tea. Delicious. The hot tea felt so good against her throat, which seemed constantly scratchy in the dusty, heavy air. She took another sip and felt something chunky in the back of her throat. She gulped it down and then gagged and almost threw it back up. Turning her body away from the table, she coughed and took a drink from her water bottle. This time Kiano asked, "You are okay, Hannah?"

"Yes, I'm sorry. The tea was just a little hot," she explained as she wondered what in the world that could have been. It was milk straight from the cow and had chunks in it. *I'll ask Mom later.* In the meantime, she worried about her lame excuses after choking twice during one meal. *I think they're on to me.*

They all helped clear the dishes from the table. Between the tight space and no light, they bumped into each other a few times. Dani, Meredith, and Beatrice used rags and a bucket of water to clean the dishes, and then Kiano and his family wished everyone a good night and went home. "See you tomorrow at Harvest Festival!" Hannah called out as they left.

With permission from Dani to use the gas lamp, Wilkister took Hannah to get ready for bed. Wilkister's brothers had already changed and gotten into their bed in the same room. Wilkister's little sister would sleep out on the couch with her dani and Hannah's mom would sleep on the other couch.

Hannah climbed in under the bed net while Wilkister went to return the gas lamp to Dani. As Wilkister found her way back in the dark, Hannah felt uneasy about sleeping in the bed with the bed net while everyone else slept in other beds and on couches.

Despite being told several times by the boys to go to sleep, Hannah and Wilkister talked and giggled into the night.

The rooster crowed right on schedule. Hannah rolled over. "You know, Wilkister, we could probably sleep more and still make it to town with plenty of time before Harvest Festival. Is there anything we can do to train him so he stops now and crows again in an hour?" Hannah shifted again, wishing there was a rooster snooze button. Wilkister did not move. Hannah leaned over and gave her a playful shove. "You know what I mean? Train the rooster to let us sleep longer?"

Wilkister sat up—dizzy—and then lay back down.

"Are you okay, Wilkister?"

"Yes, yes, I am fine. We need to milk cow now."

"I can milk it while you rest," Hannah said.

Wilkister laughed so hard she started coughing.

"Are you okay?"

Wilkister waved her hand at Hannah and said, "Yes, I fine. Is just funny. You milk cow is funny. Let us go."

They walked outside to milk the cow. The barn had a tin roof and was made of branches, wire and sod. Knowing Hannah had never milked a cow before, Wilkister grabbed a wooden stool and a tin bucket and approached the mooing cow. She said, "You need to put this on cow udder and then is okay to milk." Hannah watched as Wilkister applied a thick oil to the cow's udder. *Gross.* "Then you do like this." Hannah watched hoping Wilkister would just finish it herself, but she stood up and directed Hannah to the stool. Hannah giggled, sat on the stool and start milking. Trying not to gag, she used just her index fingertips and thumbs. Wilkister's amusement made Hannah laugh, too, but then Wilkister started to cough again. She wiped the sweat from her forehead.

"Are you sure you're all right, Wilkister? And, am I almost done here?"

Wilkister laughed and coughed. "Yes, I okay—and no, you are not almost done." She delighted in watching her friend finish milking the cow even though she was coughing and sweaty.

When they walked back inside, the boys were already

gone. Wilkister said she was going to lie down for a few more minutes while Hannah got ready. *Got ready?* Hannah reached for her shirt. It reminded her of spin art from kindergarten when they would insert paper, pour colors into the plastic piece in the middle, crank the lever around and around, and artwork would appear. She remembered the random spattering of colors. Instead of paint, her shirt was spattered with bug guts. All over. They were dried out and hardened, unpredictably patterned. What once had been a white shirt was now covered with a layer of the reddish clay dirt and sprinkled with bug remains. She put it on anyway. It was the coolest shirt she had and she would rather have a little relief and bug crust than wear another t-shirt she had brought on the trip that was cleaner. It was black to detract bugs and keep her cool at night. *Detracting bugs? Cool at night? What was I thinking?* She put on her long navy skirt, splashed water from her water bottle on her face, used a bit of it to brush her teeth, sprayed her head with Deet, and was ready for the day. She went over to the bed, lifted the bed net and nudged her friend.

"Kister? Are you ready to get up? I want to be there this afternoon by the time all the kids get there and you promised to take me with you to fetch the water. Wilkister?" Wilkister was silent. Hannah ran to the kitchen where her mom and Dani were having tea and cried out, "Wilkister is sick."

Dani, aged and frail, hobbled hurriedly into the small

dirt floored room, kicking up a dust ball. Evelyn wobbled behind her. The bed net got tangled as Dani pushed her way through. "Kister?" Wilkister's whole face glistened with sickly sweat. As her dani touched her face, they all heard Wilkister sigh. She opened her eyes and sat up, then fell back and fainted.

Dani moved to the side so Hannah's mom could get a close look at Wilkister. She felt her forehead, looked at her hands and arms, and gently lifted her eyelids to check her eyes. She looked back to Hannah and asked her to get the cell phone. Hannah ran to her mom's bag, grabbed the phone and tried to call Dr. Omundo. "There's no reception!" she yelled. She went outside the wood-slat door and tried again. Nothing. She ran back inside.

"She usually not so bad like this," Dani said, crying softly. "She usually okay but just not feel good."

"Do you have any medicine here?" Hannah's mom asked. Dani shook her head.

"I need to go to the clinic. Right, Mom?" Hannah asked. "I need to get her medicine."

"I go with you," Dani added.

Hannah looked at Dani moving so slowly and whispered to her mom. "But I need to go fast, right?" *But I'm afraid to go alone.*

"I'll go with you, Hannah," her mom said. She got up from the bed and took Hannah's arm. "We'll run together."

"But you need to stay with Wilkister."

Her mom took Hannah by the arm and led her to the kitchen. She whispered, "We don't know everyone here. And I want to be trusting. But I can't. Not with you. Not when it comes to your safety. You can't run all the way to the clinic by yourself."

She took her cell phone, grabbed Hannah's hand and ran with her out the thin, unsecured wooden door of the Omolo's hut. She tried using her cell phone. Still no reception. She ran a little farther and dialed again. Hannah hustled behind her. "Jones? Is Dan with you?"

Hannah gasped. *Dad? With Jones?*

They waited a moment and then she heard her mom say, "Dan, we're fine. I need you to get Lariam and have Jones drive you to the edge of the maize stalks that lead out to the Omolo's hut. He knows where it is. Hannah is going to meet you there. Wilkister is very sick and it's the fastest way."

Hannah heard her dad's voice on the other end of the phone. She knew he would insist on another plan that did. not involve her.

"Okay, I am sending her now."

I was wrong.

Her mom hung up the phone. "Han, your dad and Jones are making trips back and forth from Kisumu to help get ready for Harvest Festival this afternoon. They're close to Sauri now, so they'll be there to meet you by the time you run out to the edge of the corn stalks where

Jones dropped us off. It's not far and you're right—it would be best for me to stay here. And Dad has medicine for Wilkister. He brought it with him from home."

Hannah smiled. *My big surprise.*

"You need to get there fast, Hannah. Are you sure you remember the way?"

"Yes," she lied.

A Calf Named Brian Higgins

Her face tear-lined and sweaty, Hannah raced into the maize fields. She was nervous she might not remember the way and would get lost for longer than it would take Dani to walk.

She looked around. There were maize stalks, empty dirt paths, and some bushes and trees. Everything looked the same. Her conversations with Wilkister had always been so entertaining that she just walked alongside her friend and chatted, never feeling the need to learn the route since she never imagined she would have to go by herself. *I should have paid more attention.*

Her breath unsteady from starting and stopping, she ran at full speed and then slowed down to get her bearings. She could run a seven-minute mile. With the thickness of the maize and her uncertainty of direction, she figured on an eight-minute mile. Maybe nine.

As she ran, she recognized certain landmarks—a break in the rows of maize where she would turn right to get onto a dirt path that should, if she remembered correctly, lead directly to the outskirts of the stalks. She thought of landmarks used at home—turn right at the second stop light, watch for a CVS on your left. She used road signs and GPS navigation systems that would redirect her if she had made a wrong turn. Hannah's dad, like Hannah, had a horrible sense of direction and when driving somewhere would always leave enough time for the GPS to reprimand him several times for making wrong turns. They would laugh that the voice, even though they knew it was a recording, would seem to get more and more irritated every time it would say, "Recalculating!"

Hannah was not laughing now. She would give anything to hear that annoying voice say, "Destination one mile, on left," just to confirm she was going in the right direction.

As she continued to run, stop, and look from side to side to get her bearings, strands of her hair stuck against her hot face, sticky with a mixture of dust and sweat. Reaching back to pull her elastic tighter, she realized she had lost it along the way. She screamed in frustration.

She continued along the dirt road, her hair in her face. The sun throbbed, trash burned, goats passed by. The smell was only bearable because she knew she had to get medicine for her friend. Estimating she left around 5:45 a.m., she had no idea what time it was or how long she had been running. And she was exhausted.

Looking around again, she panicked. *Where am I?* At least her dad had Jones with him. She had no one. And she wanted her mom to stay with Wilkister. She had insisted.

She heard a rustle in the stalks of maize. *Never go anywhere alone.* She stopped and was quiet. She held her breath. *Was it a goat? A snake?* She thought back to her conversation with Wilkister on the bus. *It couldn't be a lion.* The rustles got louder and her heart pounded. She huddled down to hide. From between two full stalks of maize, a stranger approached her. She remained still as she looked up and into his brown eyes.

The intensity of the African sun created a silhouette around the man's head and narrow shoulders. Old, with deep creases in his weathered dark skin, he shuffled up closer to her. He was tall and grasped a carved wooden stick that came up to his mid-torso. His clothes were ragged. A button-down tattered shirt streaked with clay dirt was missing a middle button, and his shin-length pants looked as though they were originally tan, but had turned dark brown with wear and were too large against his lean body. He wore black rubber sandals.

His knees cracked loudly as he used his cane to balance and squatted in front of her. "You are Hannah Higgins," he said.

"Yes," she confirmed. She stayed still and stared at the ground.

"Your uncle was a good man." She looked up. His eyes—warm and chocolate-brown—were directly at her level. His beard of whiskers was pure white and matched his head of short textured hair. He smiled.

He was missing several teeth. Trying not to stare, Hannah looked down at her lap. She brushed at her skirt.

"You knew my uncle?" she asked.

"I know your uncle to many years. I meet him first time he come to Sauri, and I here when would be his last visit to us. We grateful to him, Hannah."

"Thank you," she said. She had not taken any water with her and the sun was beating down. Trash burned in the distance and the smell overwhelmed her.

She thought of Wilkister and began to cry. "Can you help me, please? I need to get to the edge of the stalks, not far from the clinic. My friend Wilkister has malaria and needs medicine. I thought I was close but now I think I'm lost."

"Yes, of course," he said. "Walk with me." He used his cane to straighten himself as he stood back up.

"Sir?" she said gently. "I need to get there fast."

"Okay, look to here." He pointed his cane in the distance and said, "You go this way to one half kilometer and you see clinic from maize stalk."

She stood next to him to angle herself perfectly in the

direction he was pointing. "Asante," she said and ran off.

"Hannah?" He called to her. She looked back at him while jogging backwards into the stalks. "My calf is named Brian Higgins."

"What?" Hannah asked.

"Your uncle care to us. He brought to us medicine and tell to us how use it. He helped to us harvest our land. He started community food program in our village so no more death from hunger. He changed our lives, Hannah. My calf is named Brian Higgins."

Hannah stopped running. Her mouth dropped open and she took a deep breath in. Her head tilted to one side. She looked at him smiling at her, exhaled and smiled back. *A calf named Brian Higgins? His calf is named Brian Higgins?*

She cheered. "Thank you! Asante sana, Sir!" He laughed and motioned her to go on ahead and she ran with confidence. She had never been so proud.

Seeing a break in the stalks up ahead, her pace increased. She was feeling lightheaded, but she kept running. She tripped and smacked onto the red clay dirt, still moving forward. Feeling like she was on a dry Slip-N-Slide, her body dragged along the bumpy dirt.

When she finally stopped being propelled forward, she sat up and looked at her throbbing right ankle. It was red and swollen. There was no ice, no water. She lay there, exhausted. Then she thought of the calf named Brian

Higgins and got a burst of energy. She rubbed her swollen ankle gently and got up. A goat passed her and made her laugh. She jogged ahead clumsily, favoring her injured side. She ran through the edge of the stalks. With no sign of Jones or her dad, she continued hobbling toward town.

"Dr. Omundo!" she called out when she saw him riding his bike toward the clinic.

"Hannah! What is happen?" he called back as he pedaled quickly to her.

"It's Wilkister. She's really sick. She needs medicine for her malaria."

Dr. Omundo helped Hannah onto the back of his bike and they rode quickly—boda-boda style—toward the clinic. The bike hit a rock, launching them onto the ground. "I sorry, Hannah. You are okay?" He got up and hustled toward her.

"Yes, I'm fine," she said. She stood up and wiped her hands on the side of her skirt. They walked back to the bike. It had a flat tire. *There are no bike stores, no air pumps or supplies to fix it.* She looked up at Dr. Omundo with big tears in her eyes.

"We leave bike, find your dad and get to Wilkister, quick," he declared.

His sense of urgency worried Hannah. *Can you die from malaria? We have to get back to her.* Squinting her eyes, Hannah saw a man riding a bike not too far in the distance. "Is that Mr. Awour?" she asked.

"Yes. Julius!" Dr. Omundo called out. "We borrow to your bike, is okay?"

"Yes, yes, of course. What it is?" He rode to them and passed his bike to Dr. Omundo.

"Wilkister Omolo need medicine now," he answered.

"You take. Is okay."

They thanked him and Dr. Omundo pedaled toward town with Hannah riding on the back.

"Dad!" Hannah jumped off the back of the moving bike and ran into her father's arms. She hugged him tightly and whispered, "Thank you, Dad." Smiling, he picked her up, swung her around, and then put her down. "Ouch." She winced.

Her dad looked down at her ankle. "What happened? Are you okay?"

"Yes, I'm fine. Wilkister's not, though," she said.

Her dad patted his right front pocket. "I have the Lariam. Let's go. Jones, will you take us to Wilkister?"

"Yes, is good." They put Mr. Awour's bike in the back of the truck and drove as far as they could to the Omolos, picking up the bike with a flat tire along the way. They parked at the edge of the corn stalks. Dr. Omundo took the Lariam, and he and Hannah continued on Mr. Awour's bike while Jones and Hannah's dad hurried behind on foot.

Dr. Omundo and Hannah got to Wilkister's hut and ran inside. Dani was crying in the kitchen. "Wilkister in her room, still not wake." She sniffed. "Asante," she repeated again and again.

Hannah's mom was under the bed net with Wilkister. She had taken a wool blanket from the other room and covered her. A wet cloth was draped over Wilkister's forehead.

Dr. Omundo sat Wilkister up in bed and gave her the medicine with water. He helped her lie back down and put the wet cloth back on her head. Hannah's mom got out from under the bed net and went to Hannah who was sitting down in the corner of the room with her head between her knees.

"Here, Hannah. Take this water." She held Hannah's head while she sipped the water from a bottle. Her mom gasped. "What happened to your ankle? It's all red and swollen." She looked around. "Where's Dad?"

"I fell. It looks sore, but it's fine. I can walk on it." Her mom examined Hannah's ankle. "Dad's with Jones. They'll be here any minute. Dr. Omundo and I had a bike."

Her mom walked over to the couch and got the other blanket. She folded it to prop up Hannah's foot. Her ankle throbbed and the wool blanket felt scratchy against her exposed skin.

Hannah began to guzzle the water and it quenched her thirst only a bit. The more she drank, the thirstier she became. She envisioned the poster of the human body and its organs on the wall of her science classroom, only in this version she saw her own body, and her lungs were filled with red clay dirt. Picturing the poster, she recalled it was right next to the one about thinking like a proton and staying positive. She shut her eyes and remembered Uncle Brian in her science classroom talking to her classmates and teacher. Tears seeped through her closed eyes. *I zinc I love you so much, Uncle Brian.*

Just as she finished drinking, she threw the water back up. Her mom told her to stay there, that she would get water and a cloth to clean it up. Hannah sighed. Sitting there with her vomit seeping into the dirt next to her, she felt better.

Final Preparations

On the drive back to Kisumu, Hannah stared out the front of the truck, numb to the unpaved roads. She put her head on her dad's shoulder for a moment, but it was too bumpy. She looked up at his face, a grey-green shade, sweaty and dirty. She took his hand. He looked at her and smiled. "When did you get here?" she asked.

"I stayed with Patrick and his family last night because I didn't want you to find out I was here. He showed me the ICRAF Center and that's where I met Jones. I brought medicine from Mom's friends at the hospital and, after you told me about Kiano needing glasses, I asked my friends at work to bring in old eyeglasses. I went to our eyeglasses place at home to see if they had any and they gave me several pairs and a lensometer to read the prescriptions.

Dr. Omundo knows how to use it!" Hannah nestled into him while he talked.

They pulled into the Classic. Hannah's mom had called and told Grace what had happened in Sauri. Grace and Ash were outside to greet them when they arrived.

"Hannah!" Grace called out. She hugged her and asked, "You will help me bake cake? And I need to go one time to market. You take boda-boda with me, is okay?"

"Sure." She went upstairs, put her backpack in the room, tied her hair back with the orange ponytail holder she had kept safely tucked away in her toiletry bag, took out her elephant purse and went back downstairs.

"Meredith, you watch cake. Is bake and then we make frosting. We need more sugar at market."

"Can Dad come?" Hannah asked. She looked over at her nauseous father. He nodded his head and walked with them out to the street while her mom stayed behind.

Grace called out for three boda-bodas to the market. Hannah told her dad about balancing on the back of the bikes and Uncle Brian eating too much nyoyo. Picturing him giggling at them as he watched from heaven, she looked up into the sky and smiled. Her bike and Grace's were ahead of her dad's. She glanced back and saw him wobbling off the back. The rider was struggling. "I haven't even had nyoyo yet!" he called out to Hannah. "How could I have eaten too much?" Hannah laughed.

As the riders pedaled to the market, Hannah thought

of the two boda-boda drivers who cheered with their US dollars. She thought of Kiano's uncle as they passed the Mon Ami Club. "That's the Mon Ami Club, Dad! See?"

He gave a thumbs up and lost his balance. The rider stopped and her dad got off the back of the bike. The rider then steadied it and her dad got back on. As Hannah watched him, she thought how strange it was for a kid to be proud of her parent. *Parents are supposed to be proud of their kids, not the other way around. But look at him. He would never have done this in a million years if he didn't love me so much. And Uncle Brian.*

They arrived at the market and Grace said, "I be just quick, sweet Hannah." She hurried ahead to a cart with burlap sacks of sugar.

Hannah and her dad wandered around the tent with all kinds of wooden masks and statues, Maasai bead bracelets and belts. She congratulated him on his first successful boda-boda ride and told him about the boys and the US dollars, the wooden carved cell phone Eliud made for her, and the basket her classmates and teachers had given to her. Her dad pointed to a giant giraffe mask like one Uncle Brian had bought for him. Out of the corner of her eye, Hannah spotted a wooden carved calf. She asked her dad to stay where he was and not look in her direction. Hustling over to it, she greeted the man and asked how much it cost. "200 shillings," he answered. *Less than $3.*

Hannah reached into her elephant purse and gave

him the money. He handed her the calf and she smiled. "Asante sana," she said, tucked it in the back of her skirt to hide it and ran back over to her dad.

"What was that all about?"

"You surprised me. I want to keep this as a surprise for you," she answered. He put his arm around her and they went to find Grace.

When they got back to the Classic, her dad went upstairs to lie down. He called out to her, laughing. "Beary looks ridiculous under that bed net, Hannah!"

"He's protected from the mosquitoes!"

Hannah told Grace and her mom all about the old man with a calf named Brian Higgins. She showed them the wooden carved calf and said she would give that to her dad when she told him the story of the calf named after his brother.

They frosted the cake and waited for Jones to return from his final errands to take them back out to Sauri for Harvest Festival. Ash batted his eyelashes hoping for some frosting.

Harvest Festival

Harvest Festival had finally arrived. Everyone in the village—kids, adults, boys, girls, men, women, the entire community—had waited for this day, the first annual celebration of no one in the village dying of hunger for an entire year.

The children at Bar Sauri Primary School had prepared dance routines. Nyoyo was served. Swing Swing played on a radio. The man with a calf named Brian Higgins stood at a distance watching the celebration, his calf next to him.

"I forget something, Hannah. I need go back at Kisumu."

"You can't go now, Jones. It's going to take too long. You'll miss the entire party."

"You see. I come back very soon," he smiled and winked at her.

"My dad is here. That is the biggest gift ever. We have nyoyo for everyone, the cake Grace made, the singing and dancing. Hector is here. What else could we possibly need?" She looked up at him. "I just want you to be here, Jones. That's all I want."

Jones kissed the top of her head and jogged to his truck.

The singing and dancing continued. Hannah took a bite of her nyoyo and thought of Uncle Brian's story about finding a worm in his. *As long as it's cooked, it counts as protein*. She laughed and wished he was there. She felt like he was.

Grace had baked an enormous cake. She cut slivers in order to feed everyone there. Many of the adults had brown and yellow teeth, but their smiles were brighter than any she had ever seen. *I hadn't even thought about dentists.*

Kiano walked up to Hannah and said he had a present for her. "You do?" Hannah asked.

"Yes, is this," he said and handed her a blue beaded bracelet with the letters HH weaved in orange beads. There were two snaps at the end that fastened it. Hannah looked up at Kiano, smiled, and hugged him. "Thank you so much, Kiano. I love it!" As she put it on, she asked. "You made this?"

"Yes." He paused. "Well, I have help from Wilkister."

"I love it, Kiano." She kissed him on the cheek. He put his head down, but she could see he was smiling.

Wilkister and Dani were walking in the distance. Hannah and Kiano ran to them. "How are you feeling, Kister?"

"Okay," she answered. "But I do not want to miss Harvest Festival or miss say goodbye to you, Hannah. And I have necklace for Emily." She pulled it out of the pocket of her purple dress and handed it to Hannah.

"You finished it!" Hannah hugged her again. "Thank you, Wilkister."

There was a hush over the crowd. Announcements were about to begin. Hannah ran over to her mom and dad, who were standing with Dr. Omundo and Beatrice. She scanned the crowd. Kiano came running up to her and Wilkister hurried behind him, out of breath. They stood on either side of Hannah and each took one of her arms.

This was Christmas morning, her birthday, and her memories of time with Uncle Brian all rolled up into one. They all gathered around. The large group was densely squeezed together. She spotted Jones in the distance. She caught his attention and waved. The air was still and the dust collected around them. Hannah thought of Pig-Pen from the Snoopy cartoons.

Anne Odhiambo got everyone's attention. "This visitor come all the way from Nairobi. I introduce to you from Kenya Parliament, Sarah Oloo, Chief Architect of the Ministry of Roads and Public Works!" The crowd cheered. Hannah gasped.

Sarah Oloo walked up to the front of the school smiling. Hannah's jaw dropped. She stared in disbelief. Sarah Oloo began talking. "Jambo!" The crowd cheered again. "I am here today because of you. Today is celebration of no more dying of hunger." She paused and choked back tears. "Today is also beginning to celebrate no more dying in motor vehicle accidents." She walked through the crowd to Hannah, shook her hand and said, "Jambo, Hannah. I am pleased to meet you again." Handing her a pair of scissors, she said. "Follow me. Please." Hannah walked with her, her parents and friends in a cluster behind. Wilkister and Kiano ran up to the front to walk with Hannah.

"What's going on?" Hannah whispered as they walked.

Shrugging their shoulders and throwing up their hands, they answered, "We do not know." She looked behind her. Her parents were with Jones, Hector, Grace, and Patrick. They were all smiling.

They walked beyond the school grounds to a dirt path. There was a brown sign with a bright purple ribbon on it. Sarah Oloo took Hannah's hand. "We are building a road from Sauri to Yala, where Brian Higgins's bus flipped, killing him, all the other passengers and the driver, because," she paused and took a breath. "Because there was insufficient road construction." *Insufficient road construction. Our meeting did make a difference.*

Regaining her composure, Sarah Oloo continued talking. "This road is called Higgins Road and construction begin today." Everyone cheered and she whispered to Hannah to cut the ribbon.

Hannah tapped Sarah Oloo on the shoulder and whispered in her ear. "Can Wilkister cut it, too?" Sarah Oloo nodded. Hannah's dad lifted her up to reach the sign. Jones lifted Wilkister. Behind the ribbon, she saw white lettering on the brown sign "Higgins Road". *Uncle Brian, this is for you.* They each took a handle of the scissors and counted. "1—2—3!" They pushed the handles together and sliced the ribbon. Hannah's cheeks blushed and tears filled in her eyes as she looked at everyone clapping and cheering. Her dad let her down and she ran over to Sarah Oloo and hugged her. Little Eluid made his way up through the crowd and hugged Hannah. Sarah Oloo watched with a wide and proud smile.

From the center of the crowd, Anne Odhiambo called out, "Asante, Sarah Oloo! And now we go back to school for more dancing!"

Hannah walked arm in arm with her parents, with Kiano, Wilkister and Eliud beside them. Sarah Oloo was walking close by. Hannah ran over to her. "Thank you for honoring my special uncle."

Sarah Oloo put her arm around Hannah. "It is you,"

she corrected. "You have honored your special uncle." She emphasized "you".

Hannah looked up at her and smiled. "We both have. And Wilkister."

They returned to the school and Hannah stared back at the sign for Higgins Road. She could not believe it.

Patrick said a prayer for Uncle Brian.

Dr. Omundo walked up to Hannah's dad and thanked him for the lensometer. "Kiano!" Hannah exclaimed. "You'll be able to see the labels." He grinned and asked Dr. Omundo if he could go see him tomorrow. Dr. Omundo patted him on the head and nodded.

Kiano's mom handed a note to Hannah's mom, hugged her, hugged Hannah, and walked away. Hannah's mom opened the folded paper—white with patches of red and brown dust and meticulous handwriting in pencil.

Hallow Mrs. Meredith Higgins,

It is a granted opportunity to have you teach me in clinic and talk to my new friends from America. I thank you for taking all of your time to help those who are unable to at least be sure of their future. This my first time to do work since my school. And to that I appreciate your communication. With that I may learn something in my life that I can be proud of. In another word, I am better be good at something other than be good at nothing. With all these I hereby remain.

Yours faithfully,
Beatrice Olouch

Hannah's mom ran to catch up with Beatrice and hugged her. Clutching the letter in her hand, she said, "This is my best gift. You taught me."

Hannah looked out to the crowd and saw the village elder with his calf. She ran over to him. "Sir?"

Using his cane for balance, he turned to face her. "Hannah," he said softly. "You are so good. You bring joy to us, same as your uncle."

"*You* bring joy to *me*," she articulated. "You named your calf after my Uncle Brian."

He smiled and patted his calf standing next to him. "This Brian Higgins."

Hannah giggled. "Would you come meet my parents and friends?"

"Yes, yes, of course," he said.

Hannah's parents walked to meet them. They greeted each other with a jambo and a handshake and the old man introduced them to his calf, Brian Higgins. Hannah had never seen her dad cry before. His shoulders shook. He covered his face and then wiped tears from his eyes. She took the wooden calf out of her pocket. "I got this for you, Dad. To remember Uncle Brian." He hugged her for a long time.

The sun began to set over Sauri.

Saying goodbye to Wilkister was hardest of all.

"You change my life, Hannah."

"No," Hannah insisted. "You changed mine."

Wilkister giggled and said, "We change each other lives."

Giggling through her tears, Hannah agreed. "We changed our lives."

Epilogue

Upon her return to the United States that summer, Hannah and her friends collected and distributed gently worn eyeglasses to people in need around the world—including in their own community. She talked to Wilkister and Kiano all the time, and Livvy and Jimmy got to meet on video. Hannah's principal worked with Anne Odhiambo to start a School-to-School video connection partnership. Though sometimes challenging because of Internet disruptions and the time difference, they managed to schedule monthly calls. The students and teachers became lifelong friends and the School-to-School partnership continued to grow throughout the years.

Wilkister sold her beaded jewelry in Kenya and—with the help of Hannah and her mom—in the United States. Using the profits, she and her siblings attended secondary school. Wilkister also attended university where she studied business. She then returned to Sauri to help establish and manage small business loans for other young people in her community, especially girls. Working as an apprentice to Sarah Oloo, Wilkister helped complete construction on Higgins Road. Both Wilkister and Kiano traveled to the United States to visit Hannah and her family. Wilkister rode a roller coaster.

Hannah studied International Development in college, during which time she traveled back to Sauri, and to Kitui, where Jones introduced her to Rebecca and Anthony. Helping build School-to-School partnerships among schools globally, Hannah wanted to give children and their teachers around the world the same opportunity she had.

Whenever Hannah heard people question the possibility of poverty ending, she thought back to her first visit to Sauri, Kenya and remembered Uncle Brian's words about the importance of progress and the value of getting to know each other. In her little elephant purse, which she still carried with her, she kept a picture of the old man and his calf. They reminded her that everything is possible. An old man and his calf named Brian Higgins.

The smiling faces of children in Sauri, Kenya.

Kisumu Airport, where it all began.

Sauri Clinic staffed with local doctors.

From this side, the toilet stalls look fine, right?

Gathering fuel to roast maize for lunch.

The author and Sauri's beautiful children.

Sauri children seeing their faces in a camera for the first time.

Jimmy's in the doghouse in Sauri.

Author's Note

I wrote this book based on my experience living in Sauri, Kenya as an adult. Almost everything in this story happened to me, including meeting the Chief Architect of the Ministry of Roads and Public Works on a flight from Nairobi to Kisumu when the bag I carried was too heavy; driving with Jones in a yellow Toyota truck; staying at the Classic Guest House with Grace and Ash; going to Bar Sauri Primary School with the children and teachers; and eating nyoyo, cow's meat, goat, Chapati, ugali, kale, and maize, and drinking milk straight from the cow. The ICRAF Center in Kisumu builds agricultural practices and sustainability efforts in developing nations and is dedicated to creating long-term change and ending poverty. Patrick, Hector, Dr. Omundo, Wilkister, Dani, Kiano, Beatrice, Eliud and the other characters are all based on people I met during my trip. I took the children beach balls and Frisbees, which were used only for special occasions. There was only one netball hoop. The clinic often did not have enough medicine and people died from preventable disease. The first Harvest Festival to celebrate one full year without anyone in Sauri dying of hunger took place when I was there in July 2005. There has been a celebration every year since because of community-based initiatives including the school lunch program. Wilkister made me a beaded necklace and all of the people in the community gave me a woven basket. Roosters crowed promptly at 5 a.m. each morning and there were wandering goats, chickens, lizards, and mysterious—large and loud—bugs. And there was an old man with a calf named Sonia Sachs, a hero in paving the road that will end global poverty.

Adopted by world leaders in September 2015, Sustainable Development Goals (SDGs)—also called Global Goals—are working toward ending all forms of poverty, fighting inequalities, and protecting our planet.

Goal 1: No Poverty
End poverty in all its forms everywhere.

Goal 2: Zero Hunger
End hunger, achieve food security and improved nutrition, and promote sustainable agriculture.

Goal 3: Good Health and Well-Being
Ensure healthy lives and promote well-being for all at all ages.

Goal 4: Quality Education
Ensure inclusive and quality education for all and promote lifelong learning.

Goal 5: Gender Equality
Achieve gender equality and empower all women and girls.

Goal 6: Clean Water and Sanitation
Ensure access to water and sanitation for all.

Goal 7: Affordable and Clean Energy
Ensure access to affordable, reliable, sustainable and modern energy for all.

Goal 8: Decent Work and Economic Growth
Promote inclusive and sustainable economic growth, employment and decent work for all.

Goal 9: Industry, Innovation, and Infrastructure
Build resilient infrastructure, promote sustainable industrialization and foster innovation.

Goal 10: Reduced Inequalities
Reduce inequality within and among countries.

Goal 11: Sustainable Cities and Communities
Make cities inclusive, safe, resilient and sustainable.

Goal 12: Responsible Consumption and Production
Ensure sustainable consumption and production patterns.

Goal 13: Climate Action
Take urgent action to combat climate change and its impacts.

Goal 14: Life Below Water
Conserve and sustainably use the oceans, seas and marine resources.

Goal 15: Life on Land
Sustainably manage forests, combat desertification, halt and reverse land degradation, halt biodiversity loss.

Goal 16: Peace, Justice, and Strong Institutions
Promote just, peaceful and inclusive societies.

Goal 17: Partnerships for the Goals
Revitalize the global partnership for sustainable development.

ARE YOU READY TO GET INVOLVED?

To take action in your daily life and contribute to a sustainable future, visit http://www.un.org/sustainabledevelopment/takeaction/

For more information about efforts to end poverty in sub-Saharan Africa and beyond, visit www.millenniumpromise.org

To set up a School-to-School connection between your school and a school in another part of the world, visit www.connecttolearn.org

For inspiration, read about Grace O'Halloran, my former math student who founded Gracie's Glasses, by visiting www.graciesglasses.org

Acknowledgements

When my publisher told me there would be space at the end of my book to thank people who helped along this adventure, I lost sleep. I did not know how it would be possible to express my gratitude to all the people who have inspired me, encouraged me, and loved me along the way. I spent eleven and a half years on and off writing this book, after all! A few days later, I was at a Westport Writers' Workshop meeting where I asked for guidance and a fellow writer asked if I had heard Maureen Stapleton's 1982 Oscars acceptance speech in which she thanked everyone she had ever met in her entire life. I smiled and exclaimed, "That's what I want to do!"

To my parents, Bill and Mary Lou; my sweet dog, Livvy; my nephews and nieces David, Samantha, Caroline, Courtney, Meghan, and William; my siblings Caryn and Geoff; my brother-in-law and sister-in-law, Dave and Allison; and Cousin Mike,—this would never have happened without you! To my entire family and all of my friends; the angels watching over who will always be with me, many of whom were part of the adventure of writing this book; and Shawn Mishler for our countless long talks over Tuskers and Fanta orange sodas and all our many friends in Sauri and Kisumu who treated us as family from the moment we arrived. Thank you all for loving me so much.

Thank you, Keith Garton, for your lifelong friendship filled with laughter and love. You have been my friend and mentor since the day we met so many years ago and I am incredibly proud to have Red Chair Press as the publisher of my book. Your guidance, patience, expertise and humor during its production have meant the world to me. Throughout the long process of writing, I would often tell people that I write a solid research paper and a lovely thank you note—I don't know how to write a book, but I have a story to tell. I am thankful that I finally finished writing the book after all these years and I am overwhelmed with appreciation to you for making it possible for me to tell my story.

Its main character is named after Hannah Sachs, who was in my fourth-grade class during the 2004 Presidential Election. In an election project addressing national and world issues, Hannah motivated our entire class to work toward ending global poverty, beginning with an increased awareness and a deeper understanding of the issue. Though only nine years old at the time, Hannah's passion for making our world a better place inspired me to travel and to learn. The summer after her fourth-grade year, I had a dream-come-true opportunity to live in Sauri, Kenya on behalf of the wonderful work of her parents, Jeff and Sonia. Hannah and her family changed my life and I am so blessed to have them as my friends.

So when I think back to all of the people who have influenced this story, I have to take a page from Maureen Stapleton and thank everyone I have ever met in my entire life—all of you have been so good to me and I am truly grateful!